Toward Two Words

by Orlando Bartro

Smits & Prins Publishing Company

Library of Congress Control Number: 2016907213

hardcover edition:
ISBN-13   978-0-9980075-2-6
ISBN-10   0-9980075-2-8

paperback edition:
ISBN-13 978-0-9980075-0-2
ISBN-10 0-9980075-0-1

1. Fiction, literary

Hardcover and paperback drawing by Eveline Tarunadjaja. The electronic edition may have a different cover drawing.

Printed in the United States of America.

Smits and Prins Publishing Company
Pittsburgh, Pennsylvania

Publication date: February, 2017

Toward Two Words

1. The box
2. He usually misunderstands most of it
3. Another understandable misunderstanding
4. The remaining possibility
5. He isn't prepared for this conversation
6. Doing the impermissible
7. It shouldn't be the same
8. Is this how it is?
9. They are still wearing the same clothing
10. Pretending to know
11. This may happen in a bedroom
12. This refers to what was said before
13. Does she always change her voice like that?
14. This could have been different, too
15. Or is pretending not to
16. To escape without seeming to
17. Not this! Not this!
18. Sufficiently to be convincing
19. It happened, now explain it
20. He never uses *pair* in this context
21. Obviously, bluebirds can't be seen in a green tree
22. Not yet the end
23. He should be elsewhere
24. The sofa

Toward Two Words

1. The box

To escape from the most terrifying of the monsters, Matthew Mathelson withdrew to a balcony to sleep on a sofa under the moon. He hadn't slept well for months. He was only thirty-three, but he was more anxious than an old man who has forgotten where he lives. Though the hotel was unusually quiet, and though the doors of the adjacent restaurant were closed, he doubted he could sleep. But he fell into a dream, though even of this he wasn't certain.

He woke when someone touched his head.

"Who's there?" he cried.

"It's appeared in the grove," said a man, who in the darkness was nothing but a twitching mustache. "They say it's the ghost of your father."

Matthew had seen this man doing small jobs here and there throughout the hotel, and he knew him to be a jokester.

"I won't say that's impossible," said Matthew slowly, "but you shouldn't have woken me."

"They say the ghost wants to speak with you."

"Why would my father come to see me here?" asked Matthew, not believing the man's story, and yet feeling as though something about it was true, or at least threatening. But he dismissed it again as a joke.

"Speak with the ghost yourself," he said. "I'm trying to sleep."

"Here? On a sofa? You think that's appropriate?"

Matthew considered sleeping on the sofa no more than a minor impropriety, but he nevertheless swung himself to his feet.

The man with the mustache turned away with a satisfaction that suggested he had been victorious.

Matthew, however, refused to acknowledge the man's victory, and with all the dignity that he thought he ought to have possessed, he withdrew into the hotel and descended a staircase to his room.

His room was not much larger than a closet, and it was shaped like a box. He disliked living in a box because rectangles are evidence of the presence of human beings, the most terrifying of the monsters. But he had made the room his own, and he had accepted it as his refuge, away from ghosts and human beings, where he could be alone except for two items of furniture. His bed was squeezed between the walls, and at its foot, beside a window, stood a tall cabinet that seemed to watch him. Behind its double doors were many drawers, of different sizes, in which he had organized his possessions.

Otherwise, the room was bare except for a drawing of a parrot, which hung at the upper corner of the wall, where nobody could reach it easily. The drawing had been a gift from his son. It was crudely drawn, as children's drawings usually are, but it contained no rectangles, which pleased Matthew as much as the gift itself. His son was apparently growing into a gifted young man, despite the influence of his mother, who saw the boy only occasionally. A month after birthing him, she had left him to be raised by her aunt. Matthew had visited his son once a month, which was as often as he had been allowed. He would have preferred to have visited more often, or even to have raised the boy himself, but unfortunately, his influence over him had been insignificant.

Matthew knew that he had to write a message to his son, but he preferred to delay unpleasant tasks. He even refused to do them in the hope that they would become unnecessary. But the appearance of his father's ghost having reminded him of a father's duties, he lay on his bed and wrote in a notebook:

"Dear son, if you think I'm too obvious, remember that spontaneous applause is rarely given to an actor in a play, but is guaranteed for a horse that walks onstage. Let me be the obvious horse to help you applaud what you otherwise might not. When I was nine years old, I wouldn't have understood this message, either. My challenge is to tell you without telling you, so we can both pretend I never told you anything."

He had tried to write this message many times, but he had always written around what he wanted to say. He rejected everything he had written, and started again.

"Dear son, you were born on an early December morning, and since that day I've been waiting without knowing why. But now the pigeons have entered through a hole in the roof of the hotel, and management has ordered that they be evacuated and the roof repaired. Somebody must be blocking this order, for reasons nobody admits knowing, because the pigeons are still there. They coo like cuckoo clocks in all the children's books, but you probably won't believe me. I don't yet believe this myself. I only know the story I'm telling myself about why people do what they do to me."

Matthew rejected this message also. He would have attempted approaching his subject from yet another angle, but it was late. He should have been asleep and dreaming.

2. He usually misunderstands most of it

Nobody knew Matthew Mathelson, nor did he know himself. But he knew his job title at the Polka Dot Hotel, which was a transformed old mansion that had once been known as the Mansion of Left Turns, nestled in the mountains near the small town of Greenburg. He was the Hospitality Head at the hotel, responsible for every possible care that conduced to a guest's feeling welcome and satisfied, but he wasn't satisfied with being only a Hospitality Head by the age of thirty-three. He had higher aspirations.

He was an actor in his daily interactions. His thoughts were as unknown to others as the moon golems were unknown to those who had birthed them through the methane canisters, as described in the *Journey to the Lair of the Moon Golems*, one of Matthew's favorite novels, and one which he had read many times, though never fully understanding it. To his subordinates, he appeared in command of himself and of them, able to make decisions decisively, and able to overcome even the most unbearable situations. Though he was occasionally severe, he was always ready to excuse the failures of others more readily than his own. Of himself he expected perfection. He had learned much during his years of employment. He knew when to twitch his eyebrows, when to scratch his lip, when to cough into the crook of his elbow, and when to scrape a hair off his tongue with his teeth. He had spoken in thousands of conversations, had memorized hundreds of useful expressions. He had begun combing his hair.

But though nine years had passed since he had met Roselyn Spring, the mother of his son, he was still thinking about her more than he should have been, and not thinking enough about Mr Plute, the owner of the Polka Dot Hotel. It was reputed that Mr Plute lay as if dead all day in his bed at the top of the tower, where he had grown as bald as a baby and as fat as a pregnant woman. Matthew had spoken with him once in a hallway, and he had never forgotten his voice, which was as low and bouncy as a tuba's. He had seen him subsequently only a few times from a distance, unless he had actually seen Mr Plute's twin brother, who was an occasional guest at the hotel. Otherwise, Mr Plute was only a name that sometimes appeared on documents that Matthew had to review, and a name on a document is but a word, which is no substitute for a man in the flesh. It was, therefore, a surprise when Mr Plute knocked like an announcement of death on the door of his room.

"Are you Matthew Mathelson?" he called.

"I am," said Matthew, waking in his bed and throwing the blankets off his face.

"The Events Manager has left us!" shouted Mr Plute through the door. "My birthday is coming soon! And we have nobody to manage tonight's festival!" He offered Matthew the position of the Events Manager, in addition to his current position as the Hospitality Head, and promised to double his salary.

Matthew had no experience as an Events Manager, but he assumed he could perform the job adequately because he could do nothing much to prepare for a festival that would happen that very night. He was pleased to have been selected for the position, and he regarded his new responsibilities as evidence that he would soon rise to be the Head Head, which was the top position at the hotel. He had, however, been hoping to read another chapter in the *Journey to the Lair of the Moon Golems*, a pleasure that would now have to be delayed.

3. Another understandable misunderstanding

The festival was an annual event. The laborers prepared it every spring, and they should have known what needed to be done without an Events Manager to manage them. The boy, the peacock, and the bear should have appeared, if they were to appear, regardless of anything Matthew Mathelson would direct. The singers should have known their songs, and the dancers their dances. Nevertheless, at dusk, Matthew circled the field around the hotel, where the preparations for the festival were nearing completion. He introduced himself to his laborers. He asked them to inform him of any issues that might develop during the night, and he promised to help them as much as he could.

Near a grove of pear trees, he paused. Roselyn Spring had been sitting beneath the pear trees when he had first seen her nine years ago. He had imagined her to be different than what she had become. In another nine years, she would become someone else again, and in nine years after that, she would probably become unrecognizable to everyone including her father, who might never have known her.

The preparations for the festival were fancifying his thoughts. He was almost another person while bewitched by a troupe of singers rehearsing a folksong:

> All the owls in maiden's hair
> Warn her nothing to beware,
> While she rides her crazy loon,
> Looping round the wrinkled moon . . .

Such a folksong might have appeared in a child's version of Tsao Hsueh-chin's *Dream of the Red Chamber*, one of his favorite novels. Roselyn, however, hadn't been anything like Tai-yu, the heroine of the book. He had invented her as thoroughly as an author invents a character. In another age, he may have moved with her toward "I do," the two words of the ancient marriage rite, while still intoxicated by the feelings that obscured the dangers that made this a poor decision. But at the time, he hadn't thought of any consequences beyond the satisfaction of his sensual desires. He had been made mad by the stench of the rotting pears, by the screeching parrots, by the shivering branches, and by his reading of stories, or rather, by his misreading of them, by his believing them to present possibilities that could be realized in reality. And yet, if anyone should have known the truth about Roselyn Spring, it should have been Matthew Mathelson—or Bill Robbins, as he had introduced himself to her. He should have realized that he had taken her from a book. He had approached her as if she would be Tai-yu, a heroine everyone could love. Even Tai-yu's faults were lovable. She had brushed her hair too often, for example, and she had been too sensitive, too normal in a house of monsters. Something rectangular was in the Mansion of Left Turns, and everyone accepted this except Tai-yu and Matthew Mathelson, or so it seemed.

He doubted he could be the only normal person on the planet Earth. Someone else, somewhere, living in a box that others call a *house*, or living in a room that moon golems call a *rectube*—which is a three-dimensional rectangle or box—surely others flinched at rectangles because they indicated the presence of human beings, the most fearsome of the monsters. But even if he was the only normal person in the world, he had become accustomed to other people and to their oddities. As a manager he was often pretending to be evaluating everything to ensure conformity with an ideal, but he usually acted as though everything was acceptable just as it was; otherwise, he would have been obligated to seek improvements, which would have required him to do more work. He therefore wouldn't have suggested anything to the laborers who were preparing the spring festival, even if it hadn't been too late to change anything.

The moon hadn't yet risen, but the guests were already arriving in their bird costumes. Most were costumed as parrots or crows; some as pigeons; and a few as robins, redbirds, peacocks, and swans. Many were dressed as pairs. Some wore beaks; others, bills. "Ka-who! Ka-who!" and "Peep-a! Peep-a!" were being called from all corners of the field, by hoarse human imitators of the birds in the pear grove. Many of the guests were already drunk. Matthew was the only one not wearing any other costume than his regular clothing, which, though fitting perfectly, had always been nothing but a disguise. He pocketed his hands into the rectangular pockets of his pants. If he could have pocketed the rest of his body, he would have; but his clothing provided sufficient camouflage, and he had the authoritative face of an Events Manager.

4. The remaining possibility

By the rise of night, every guest of the hotel was attending the festival. All of the hotel rooms were dark, and even the restaurants were empty.

Matthew climbed to a balcony overlooking the crowd and lay on a sofa. The sofa probably wasn't the same sofa as that on which he had lain nine years before with Roselyn Spring, but it looked the same, with the same polka dots on its upholstery. It was identical, however, not only to the other eight sofas on the balcony, but to all of the other sofas in lounges throughout the hotel.

He shouldn't have been thinking about Roselyn Spring. He wanted to remember nothing of that night, nine years ago. If he had then seen Roselyn as she now looked, he would have never imagined her to be anything but an actual person. She was now so fat that she squeezed through doorways. It was difficult to stand in the same room with her, without being pushed into a corner.

If he could have been always alone, he wouldn't have become aware of how selfish he had become. He supposed that many at the festival were as normal as he was. Perhaps everyone felt surrounded by monsters and feared rectangles, to one degree or another. Matthew wanted to shout to the crowd that he understood them, that he knew that they, too, were worried about the pigeons that had infiltrated the hotel through a hole in the roof. But his thinking was becoming disorganized. He was suddenly tired, as if a machine had turned off inside him. He should have been lying in his bed instead of on a sofa on a balcony. But he said a prayer, as was his custom before falling asleep, and as quick as an announcement of death, behold: an angel taller than the hotel. It was raising its wings as if preparing to spring into the empyrean, and it was holding aloft a machine gun.

"I go to measure Jerusalem," it said. "Do you have a measuring tape?"

Matthew wished to wake. He told himself to open his eyes; but his eyes were already opened in the nightmare, and he couldn't open them again and see the sky above the balcony. The angel was looking at him as if seeing everything that Matthew had ever dreamed. Matthew usually would have been bewildered by the angel's request, but in this situation, he thought it quite ordinary because on the previous day he had found a measuring tape in the top left drawer of the cabinet in his room, the same drawer that contained the hairbrush that Roselyn Spring had left with him after their night together. But the measuring tape was useful only for measuring small items, such as a baptismal certificate to determine if it was the same size as those issued at St Gemma Galgani Church, where his mother had supposedly had him baptized. If the angel wanted to measure Jerusalem, a longer measuring tape would be preferable. But Matthew didn't know where to find a longer measuring tape, and when the angel bent as if to swallow him, he woke.

It was night, and the festival was ongoing. A man was standing over him, and he was holding a fiery candle.

"It's appeared again," said the man. Behind the candle, he was nothing but a twitching mustache.

"What's appeared?" asked Matthew.

"The ghost of somebody's father."

"It's probably a kite in a tree."

"How should I know what it is?" asked the man, twitching his mustache as if preparing to tell a joke. "I'm telling you about the ghost because you're the Events Manager."

Matthew had wanted the additional position, but he hadn't wanted to be woken from his sleep. If he had known that being the Events Manager was going to be so tiring, he would have declined the position. How was he to be both the Events Manager and the Hospitality Head? Being the Hospitality Head already consumed more than half of his day. He would have to do less to perform in both positions, and this would reduce the quality of his performance. He might therefore lose both positions, and only because he had tried to do what had been asked of him. He refused to make another mistake. He had already taken three wrong turns in his life, always to the left, forming a rectangle and leaving him where he had started.

"I'll make an announcement," said Matthew.

"But what will you say?" asked the man with the mustache.

"I'll say it's a kite."

"But they say it's a ghost from the grave."

Matthew decided to join the crowd and ask where the ghost had been seen. If he hadn't been given new responsibilities, he wouldn't have had to worry about such issues. He didn't need more money. He spent almost nothing. His biggest expenditure was the payment he was delivering every month to Roselyn Spring, on behalf of their son. But he had accepted the new position, and he was determined to prove that he could perform better than anybody might have expected. He therefore descended from the balcony and crossed the field toward the pear grove where he assumed the ghost had been seen. He was acting as though nothing could be amiss. Even if the kite was a ghost, he didn't wish to alarm anyone by walking quickly, but everyone was noticing him, probably because he was the only person not costumed as a bird. As he neared the grove, he was increasingly convinced that something had been seen, but whether a ghost or a kite was yet to be determined.

Many were shouting, "A ghost! A ghost!"

Matthew straightened his hair with his hand because many people were watching him as if his arrival were a deliverance from heaven.

"Here he is!" their gazes seemed to announce. "A manager from the hotel! He will know what to do!"

Matthew was walking authoritatively and slowly, as if he were wearing a heavy robe. He had learned this manner of walking from Befijop in the *Journey to the Lair of the Moon Golems*. But Befijop hadn't had a crooked leg. Nor was Matthew's leg crooked like his mother's leg. His mother's leg was crooked, now and then, just like the leg of a normal person, such as when walking or when lying on a short sofa. But Matthew's leg couldn't be straightened. His leg had been crooked from as early as he could remember. If Matthew had been a moon golem, born like other moon golems from a canister on the moon, he wouldn't have suspected that his mother had crippled him. He might even have idealized women, as often happens in novels, though it was unfair to expect a woman to be as a man might dream her.

He had left home to escape his mother because her worrying about him had become intolerable.

"Why would you think you're a moon golem?" she had asked, with tears on her cheeks.

Her tears were, of course, intentional. Matthew was impervious to emotional manipulations. He wanted facts, not faces. Was he a moon golem or not? To answer this question, the descriptions of the moon golems that were contained in the available books were insufficient. Books such as the *Attack of the Moon Golems* and the *Journey to the Lair of the Moon Golems* contained physical descriptions of moon golems, and even samples of their dialogue, but neither blueprints nor technical specifications. According to these books, which purported to be fictional, the moon golems comprised only a small percentage of Earth's population, but they were numerous enough for Matthew to have probably met one, at least once in his life. But unless a moon golem knew itself to be one, and unless it introduced itself as such, Matthew's chances of distinguishing it from human beings were small.

He was a man who needed to be convinced. He knew he needed to be convinced, and he believed he was a man. He had tried to confirm that he was a man. He had examined his body in a mirror, and had compared it, part by part, with an anatomical drawing of a male homo sapiens. His exterior parts matched those of the anatomical drawing, but this was to be expected. The moon golems had been made to look exactly like human beings.

His mother scoffed at his worries. She swore to God that she had given him birth. Natural human procreation was still sometimes operative. He had not been born in the moon factories.

Matthew didn't believe anything his mother told him. How was he to be certain that the world had begun before the cuckoos had cried at midnight? He wasn't even certain he would die. That was what others had told him. Death was a rumor.

He was thinking too much. His mother had warned him of this.

"You're thinking too much, Bill," she had said.

Matthew had noticed that she had called him by a different name. This was the name recorded on his baptismal certificate, which he had found in a drawer in his bedroom. The certificate indicated that he had been baptized at St Gemma Galgani Church, on the ninth day after parturition. All was correct on the certificate except that his name, *Matthew Mathelson*, had been spelled *Bill Robbins*.

5. He isn't prepared for this conversation

If Matthew had expected to see a ghost, he would have been disappointed when he arrived at the grove, but because he had expected to see nothing unusual, he was surprised to see a young woman wearing a black hat. She approached as if wanting to ask a question. But he waved her away because she reminded him of Roselyn Spring, though only because she was wearing a hat. She was shorter than Roselyn, and her legs almost dragged along the ground when she walked, as if she couldn't be bothered even to lift them. He tried to escape her by continuing forthrightly into the grove of pear trees.

Lanterns had been hung, here and there, in the branches. It was as if Matthew had stepped into a ghost story. The parrots, perhaps believing that the lanterns were suns, were shrieking as if it were morning. Matthew dutifully looked for ghosts. It was easy to imagine them in the foliage, among the pale pears hanging like upside down skulls that were attracting fleas and fireflies. Matthew meant to be a diligent Events Manager, even when alone in a grove of pear trees lit with lanterns. But the shrieks of the parrots tempted him to forget his duties. He could have listened to the shrieks forever, though *forever* was an exaggeration, used only for rhetorical effect, such as often happens at the end of fairytales, when lovers are promised a forever happiness.

But Matthew would have preferred to be happy forever alone, though not alone forever in a white box, as has been recorded in a saint's vision of hell. Instead, he intended to enjoy his solitude while he could. If he had added all of the solitary moments that were to be left to him until death, he might have summed no more than a few days, perhaps a week. His thoughts began to fly outside the boundaries of a sentence, but a shadow moved across a tree; and when he turned, he met the young woman wearing a black hat. She had followed him into the grove.

"I didn't know who you were before," she said, pleasantly.

"Who did you think I was?" asked Matthew, quickly resuming the appearance of an Events Manager. He straightened his stance and face.

"It doesn't matter," she said. "I know who you are now!"

Matthew was already weary of this conversation. The lanterns in the foliage were glimmering green spheres. The opening sentence of the *Journey to the Lair of the Moon Golems* repeated in his thoughts:

Nothing happened that night, but the groves of Bekanti were glimmering.

He could have been reading in his rectube; instead, he had assumed new responsibilities.

"I'm Lucy Crowe," said the young woman. "Did you notice I'm wearing black to look like a crow? See my black hat?"

Matthew Mathelson suddenly became aware—as he had often suddenly become aware when talking to women—that he was a handsome man. He turned to leave, but Lucy touched his arm.

"You shouldn't leave without plucking a pear," she said.

"No, I'm leaving now," said Matthew.

"Hush!" she whispered, placing her finger on her lip, which was as plump and wrinkled as a fig. "Somebody might hear us!"

"We'd better leave then."

"You shouldn't take me so seriously," said Lucy. "Nobody can hear us."

"It wouldn't matter if they could. We're saying nothing."

"You shouldn't treat me like that. First you say one thing, and then you say another thing! You seem to think I'm a loose woman or something."

Matthew was perplexed by this conversation, but he had been engaged in similarly perplexing conversations before. He would have preferred not to be talking to anyone, and especially not to a woman who reminded him of his earliest memory of Roselyn Spring.

"I've thought of something else," said Lucy. "We could go back to the hotel."

"That's where I'm going," said Matthew. "To sleep."

"Why to sleep? I heard you've just been promoted. There could be trouble if they see you where you shouldn't be."

"I was thinking the same thing."

"Why?" asked Lucy. "Because there's never any surprises?"

"What surprises would you mean?"

"You didn't expect to meet me here, for example."

"I didn't."

"Are you implying something about me?" she asked, pushing up her black hat to better show her face, which was as smooth as candle wax, but only because she had smeared it with thick cream.

"Why assume that?" asked Matthew.

"I assume everything's about me because it usually is!"

Matthew was flustered by his recklessness. He should

have maintained the guise of an Events Manager throughout the conversation, but he hadn't been impervious to her charm, though he had been pretending not to understand her insinuations.

"If there's something you want to tell me," said Lucy, "please wait until tomorrow."

"Why tomorrow?" asked Matthew.

"What a way to talk! You act as if I'm serious!"

"I don't understand you."

"Listen—I know a place where nobody will see us."

"Here? Under the trees?"

"If I ever did such a thing, may I die on the spot!" cried Lucy. "No, another place. Besides—whatever I do, they're sure to fire me, eventually. But I can lie my way out of anything!"

"I believe you."

"And I have another trick. I need a friend to walk with me to Greenburg. Come with me through the woods, and pretend to be somebody else. It's boring to always be yourself."

"This is a special situation, is it?"

"It is," said Lucy. "Wouldn't you save somebody's life if you could? Not that this is anything so serious. But I wouldn't be proposing this, if I didn't have my reasons."

"I'm sorry, I can't help you."

"I'll let you think about it. I'm as clever as a snake. You'll be thinking about me tonight, I promise. Sweet dreams! May angels sing you asleep!"

She retreated slowly between the trees, as if expecting him to follow her. But he retreated deeper into the grove. He reviewed everything that he had said to her, and everything seemed appropriate, except for a few ambiguities.

6. Doing the impermissible

Matthew walked throughout the grove, from lantern to lantern. He should have been looking for a ghost or a kite; instead, he was thinking about Lucy and her black hat. He was mostly thinking about her black hat. Her hat was much like her words, which had been both circular and rectangular, depending on the angle at which he looked at them. Her words had been circular because they had looped back to refer to herself. They had been rectangular because they had hidden their sharp corners by always facing him. He hadn't been tricked by her pleasing manner. If he had been less experienced, he might have joined her show, but he had been in similar shows before, pushed onstage for comedies and melodramas that had been directed and staged by the women he had known.

He wanted to retreat to the pleasures of solitude, but the parrots weren't as entertaining when filtered through his annoyance at having been interrupted. He emerged from the grove of pear trees at a place other than where he had entered it. He hadn't seen a ghost. He hadn't even seen a kite.

He headed toward the hotel, but more people had arrived for the festival. He had to push through a crowd. Nobody bothered to look at him, not even to notice that he wasn't costumed as a bird. Many were too drunk to notice anything, including their own feet. In the thickest part of the crowd, Matthew could see nothing but the highest heads. Finally, he could push no farther, and had to backtrack toward a sofa that had been dropped in the mud. It appeared to be the sofa on which he had been lying on the balcony. It had the same polka dots, in the same places, but now its legs were broken, its upholstery ripped. A woman was lying on it. The wings of her peacock costume were folded over her, and her head was hanging over the bolster.

"Get off the sofa!" cried Matthew, in a tone that he intended to sound as outraged as he actually was.

But the woman pretended not to have heard him. Her mouth was wrinkled as if perpetually sucking something, or maybe she was offering to kiss him goodnight, or bite him.

Matthew looked around for someone who could help him carry the sofa back to the balcony, but not only didn't he see anybody who might be willing to help him, but he saw the other eight sofas from the balcony, lying in the mud, here and there, sideways or upside down. People were jumping on them, or lying on them, or embracing on them. The problem, he realized, was larger than himself. He couldn't have carried all nine sofas back to the balcony, even if carrying sofas was a proper function of a manager. Nor was it likely that he could remove the occupants of the sofas merely by yelling at them. His insignificance had become clearer than he was willing to acknowledge. Maybe he needed to be wearing an insignia, which would have designated him as a significant person.

He leaned over the woman's face and smelled a rotting pear from her mouth. She had probably been eating pears from the grove. Maybe she had been misidentified as the ghost.

"You're not permitted to sleep here," he said, jabbing her shoulder.

"Don't touch me," she said. "It's not your sofa. It's not your responsibility."

It was true that the Events Manager only managed special events, and therefore might not be responsible for sofas. Matthew may have been interfering with another manager's work. Maybe at that moment, a team had been sent by the Infrastructure Manager to retrieve the sofas from the field. But the woman couldn't be allowed to resist Matthew's justified command.

"I'm losing my patience," he said. He was, however,

almost willing to allow the woman to remain where she was. But to leave her on the sofa during his debut performance as the Events Manager was unacceptable. If anything were amiss, there would be consequences that he couldn't blame on others. But he was too experienced with similar situations that he had encountered in his role as the Hospitality Head to continue a fruitless effort. Nothing could be done beyond what he had attempted, and even his attempt had been foolhardy because it had never shown a hint of succeeding even at its conception.

7. It shouldn't be the same

The spring festival had escaped even the appearance of being under Matthew's management. He had reached the point where he could preserve his authority only by not exercising it. He therefore returned to the hotel. He would have returned to the balcony, but he couldn't bear to see the balcony empty of its sofas. He decided to sleep in his own bed in his own room, but when he arrived at the door of his room, he found it was open, which startled him. Had he arrived at the wrong room? Had he accidentally turned into one of the many secret passageways left over from the Mansion of Left Turns before it had been transformed into a hotel? No, it was his door. He recognized a nick on the doorknob. He pushed the door to open it farther, but an unfamiliar chair had been placed behind it, apparently to block his entrance. Not only sofas, but also chairs, had obviously been moved from their designated positions at the hotel. With more annoyance at the presence of the chair than fear of what had happened to his room, he reached forthrightly around the door, with all the authority of a manager, and pushed the chair away. It toppled noisily. The door could now be opened fully, but Matthew paused. If anyone was in his room, his presence had now been made obvious. He could have retreated to find help, but it was late; only the Hospitality Head would have been available at that hour for emergencies, and the Hospitality Head was nobody other than himself. He would have to solve the problem by himself, in his capacity as the Hospitality Head, if not in his capacity as Matthew Mathelson. He therefore swung the door open, as bravely as a child who expects to meet a ghost face to face.

The lamp by his bed was lit. All of his cabinet's drawers had been opened and emptied, and their contents had been strewn on the floor. And lying in the bed, with a blanket drawn up to her neck, was Lucy Crowe.

She was hatless, with brushed, blackish hair.

"Surprise!" she cried.

"It certainly is," said Matthew. "What are you doing in my room? You've opened my cabinet! And all of my drawers!"

"Don't be ridiculous. Why would I open your drawers?"

"To steal something."

"I don't appreciate these accusations," said Lucy. "You should be happy to see me!"

"Happy to see you? What have you done to my cabinet?"

"It needed to be rearranged."

Matthew went to the cabinet. One of its drawers, which had formerly contained toothbrushes, had been filled with damp, crumpled tissues.

"I don't appreciate this," said Matthew.

"You can put everything back, but it's better this way. How can you have your tissues in one drawer, and your hairbrush in another? And so on, and so on?"

"This is my room, not yours."

"Don't look so pleased," said Lucy, smirking as if enjoying his displeasure. "You need to appreciate what I did."

"There's nothing to do, except put it all back."

"I didn't think you were like this. Aren't you happy to see me?"

"I should have slept someplace else."

"You're angry."

"Why shouldn't I be angry?"

But Matthew quenched the anger in his voice because of his experience as a manager. Nevertheless, it might have been best to yell at her because she seemed to expect it; however, he had no wish to satisfy her expectation, and yelling at her might have encouraged her to stay in his room indefinitely because she seemed to thrive on conflict.

"I hope you're wearing clothes under that blanket," said Matthew.

"Maybe I am!" cried Lucy.

She pulled the blanket partly down, exposing a raised mole on her collarbone. The mole was as large and thick as a button, and hairy also. Matthew was not only repulsed by the mole, but repulsed by her pulling the blanket down to expose it. He was expecting further ugly surprises should the blanket farther descend, and her armpits, which were about to be exposed, would probably exude a stench that might even have been slightly nauseating. But if the lights had been off, he might have nevertheless become aroused. He might have rubbed against her, and friction would have achieved what it might. But even in the darkness, he would have smelled her. If her odors could have been dissipated, perhaps by opening the window, then he might have succeeded doing what she apparently wished, despite all obstacles, but he didn't want to embarrass her by making a suggestion that would help her become more attractive, nor did he desire to become attracted to her. He wanted only to drop asleep after a tiring day, having fulfilled the roles of two positions. He therefore attempted to excuse himself from sleeping with her. He told her it was late, but she eagerly agreed, as if he were suggesting that they shouldn't miss an opportunity. He countered that it was too late to do anything other than sleep—and added that he had hit his head while carrying a sofa.

"Oh! you hit your head! Let me help you!" cried Lucy, sitting up in bed, and letting the blanket drop, exposing her breasts, which were bigger than Matthew had expected, though they were widely spread apart, and one pointed downward, the other sideways.

Matthew had usually reacted to such sights with what might be considered a typical reaction, but he was too annoyed to feel anything but disgust.

"You should cover yourself," he said.

"Oh!" cried Lucy, with a squeal more delighted than upset. She gathered the blanket to hide most of her breasts, though still exposing their tops and the large mole on her collarbone.

"You must think I'm vulgar!" she said.

"I can't think anything because my head hurts," said Matthew. "I have to sleep, and only sleep."

He almost left the room to sleep somewhere else. He might have slept on one of the sofas in the field, or on a sofa somewhere in the hotel—if he could find one that hadn't been carried off. But to leave his room to Lucy would endanger everything he owned. She had already proven capable of trespassing; thievery was her likely next step. Furthermore, it would be unacceptable for a Hospitality Head to cede his room to an intruder.

"I don't want to be an inconvenience," said Lucy. "I'll leave tomorrow, when your head is better. Is there anything else I can do to help?"

"There's nothing you can do," said Matthew. "I feel sick."

"I feel sick, too," said Lucy. "I think I ate something bad."

"You'd be more comfortable in your own room."

"I thought you'd feel sorry for me! Instead, you want to chase me out!"

"I'm the Hospitality Head," said Matthew. "I can get you a special room that's all yours."

"Don't worry about me. I came here to keep you company."

"This isn't a good time. I'm sorry it has to be this way."

"Is something wrong with you? Is that why you want me to leave?"

"Nothing's wrong with me."

"But something's wrong with me," said Lucy. "I'm sick!"

Matthew thought she had meant *sick* metaphorically, but he was corrected when she vomited. She made no attempt to direct her vomit toward something that might contain it. She vomited just where she was, trying only to avoid her lap. A chocolatey mess sopped on the blankets. Every retch resulted in a more voluminous expulsion. Matthew was surprised her body could contain so much vomit. He would have retrieved a towel, but his towels, which had been neatly piled in a drawer, had been removed from the cabinet along with everything else, and dropped somewhere, out of view. He therefore retrieved a shirt instead, which was the first thing he saw on the floor, and tossed it to her. She patted her mouth with it, as if it were a napkin.

"That was embarrassing," said Lucy. "But we'll ignore it."

Matthew tossed her another shirt, thinking she'd use it to sponge up her vomit, but she didn't bother to catch it.

"Time to sleep," she said, wearily.

"You vomited on my bed," said Matthew. "And now you have to clean it, and leave."

"I don't want to leave. I want to sleep."

"I'm taking you to the infirmary."

The hotel had an infirmary in the basement. He told her he would take her there, and she would be treated for whatever sickness she might have, such as alcohol poisoning, which was the most likely culprit in his opinion, but he wasn't a doctor and couldn't know for certain. Dr Helen Nostram would know what to do. She was always available. She would diagnose Lucy's problem immediately, and cure her. Matthew said all this in his most soothing voice, as if he were a doctor himself. Lucy seemed to agree that his recommendation was sensible, but she felt too sick to walk.

"I can't walk," she said. "You'll have to carry me."

Matthew suspected she was lying, but he was willing to do whatever he had to do to remove her from his room, even if he had to carry her out. Her vomit would still be seeping into his bed, and his possessions would still be waiting to be replaced to their proper positions; but though she in justice should have righted these wrongs, Matthew was willing to right them himself, so long as he was rid of Lucy, permanently. He was therefore willing to agree to her suggestion that he carry her to the infirmary, but he hesitated to agree too quickly. If she suspected he was willing to do anything to be rid of her, she would have probably tormented him further; therefore, he forcefully pronounced that she could most certainly walk, and that he would never carry her one step anywhere, even to save her life. This pronouncement inspired Lucy to retch, but nothing vomited from her mouth, to her disappointment, which she disguised ineffectually. Her failed attempt to vomit, however, proved to Matthew that she would permit him to carry her out of his room, if she believed he was carrying her against his will, which she would regard as a victory more important than having him do the service itself.

"Where are your clothes?" asked Matthew.

"I don't know," said Lucy.

Matthew wasn't willing to look for Lucy's clothes, which would have required him to rummage through the mess she had made in his room; instead, he was willing to sacrifice his bathrobe, which was on a pile of his things, and obviously in view. He grabbed it and held it out to her, but she didn't take it.

"Take it!" he said, touching the bathrobe to her shoulder.

She held out her arm to allow him to dress her.

Matthew hadn't anticipated having both to dress and carry her, but as the carrying would be dependent on the dressing, he was willing to do the dressing as well, to achieve his goal of never seeing her again. He therefore pulled her arm through the sleeve of the bathrobe. She leaned forward, and he draped the bathrobe around the back of her neck. She lifted her other arm, and he pulled that arm into the other sleeve. She shifted back and forth a few times to settle the bathrobe on her frame. Matthew resented being used as a dressing aide. But he resolved that once Lucy was in the infirmary, he would avoid her forevermore.

"Now I'm going to carry you," said Matthew, with a disgust he didn't disguise.

He had expected Lucy to be heavy, but not as heavy as she was. He lifted her into his arms with a groan. As soon as she was safely in his arms, she snuggled her head on his shoulder and sighed triumphantly. But he almost dropped her when he pivoted with his burden toward the door, and her feet knocked against the wall. She didn't complain, or even seem to notice. She was smiling against his shirt. Her smile proved that she wasn't as sick as she was pretending to be, and he almost dropped her into her vomit to avenge himself. But he refrained, though not due to any considerations for her. The sooner he was rid of her, the sooner he could sleep. But removing her from his room wasn't as simple as he had supposed. His room was too small to maneuver easily within it while carrying a woman. Furthermore, she weighed more than he weighed, and by a greater margin than he would have guessed. He considered asking her to walk, now that he had lifted her off the bed, but foreknowing the futility of this request, he gripped her more tightly and forced himself to the door. His legs were trembling due to the added weight, and his limp was exacerbated. As he squeezed around the toppled chair and through the doorway, he again knocked Lucy's feet against the wall, and she cried,

"Ouch!"

She had pronounced *ouch* not as an involuntary exclamation, but as if reciting a word from a dictionary. Matthew was impervious to such obvious deceptions. He would have responded, but he was breathing too heavily to speak. He carried her straight to the stairs, as quickly as he could, anxious to be rid of his burden.

8. Is this how it is?

Matthew, in his capacity as the Hospitality Head, had occasionally interacted with the director of the hotel's infirmary, Dr Helen Nostram, an old, bony woman who was always forgetting things. Matthew regarded her as the most capable doctor he had ever met, though only because she had told him not to worry about being a moon golem. He had appreciated her show of concern and her reassuring words. She had listened to him, or she had appeared to listen to him, and she had repeated the same consoling phrases until he had felt satisfied that she could do nothing for him. He reasoned that if even a doctor couldn't conclusively distinguish a moon golem from a human being, then his doubts about his humanity were legitimate.

Dr Nostram was renowned throughout the Polka Dot Hotel for her commitment to her work. Though it was long past midnight when Matthew arrived at the infirmary with Lucy in his arms, he expected that Dr Nostram would be available to see them, and his expectation was fulfilled. She was examining a patient's chart in the waiting room.

Matthew carried Lucy to a corner of the waiting room and lowered her into a chair. He was relieved to be free of her weight. He only had to admit her to the infirmary to be free of her completely. He strode confidently to the counter, where Dr Nostram seemed to have been placed as if to resolve all of his difficulties.

"Dr Nostram," he said, "I've come to you for help."

"How do you know my name?" asked Dr Nostram, interrupting him.

"I'm Matthew Mathelson, one of your patients. Don't you remember me?"

"You can't expect me to remember everybody."

"But don't you remember? I'm the Hospitality Head.—I'm here because of an emergency!"

"The infirmary is full," said Dr Nostram, gazing at Lucy, who admittedly had nothing obviously wrong with her. "I've just sent our overflow to the hospital in Greenburg."

"If they're full," said Lucy, "you'll have to carry me back to our room."

Matthew noted that she had said *our room*, but he ignored the possessive adjective because it was absurd for her to think that she had obtained possession of his room merely by intruding herself into it. He addressed Dr Nostram more quietly so Lucy couldn't hear their discussion.

"This is a special case," he said. "I carried her down here because she vomited. And other things are wrong with her, too. I'm not a doctor. I don't know what to do. If you don't help me now, my situation will get worse. You must help me, Dr Nostram!" Matthew continued speaking, but he merely repeated the same pleas, using different combinations of words, or even the same combinations of words. But Dr Nostram had stopped listening to him.

"The infirmary is full," she said. "You might take her

to the hospital in Greenburg."

"Please, Dr Nostram," said Matthew. "Make an exception, and see her now."

"I'm sorry, but I have other patients," said Dr Nostram, pulling her hand off the counter as if retrieving it.

She retreated from the counter and vanished into a room.

Matthew was realizing that his desires were beyond what could be obtained, but he was yet unwilling to admit that his hopes had been for nothing. He would have stayed with Lucy, if he had had no other option, but he wasn't willing to stay with her until all possibilities of escape had been attempted. A door was within reach at his side. It was an ordinary door, rectangular, and therefore appropriate for being used by human beings, who are somewhat rectangular, excepting their heads. He turned toward the door not as if he wanted to escape through it, but as if the door might lead to another infirmary, where Lucy could be safely delivered. He grasped the doorknob, as if merely to toy with it. He opened the door, not abruptly, but with the firmness of one who had the right to open it. The door opened toward him, which blocked him partly from Lucy's view. She was watching him alertly, sitting upright, like a hawk about to hop into flight off a branch. She seemed to suspect that he was a rabbit who had become aware of her. He pretended to be casual and calm as he looked into a small storage room, filled with boxes and picture frames. He would have been disappointed, except at the back of the room was a ladder to a trapdoor in the upper left corner of the ceiling, probably one of the many secret passageways left over from the Mansion of Left Turns before it had been transformed into a hotel. He pretended, however, to have found another section of the infirmary, and he announced to Lucy that he would return for her after speaking with the other doctor at the hotel, "who was almost as good as Dr Nostram."

Matthew, however, might have spoken too eagerly because a shade of suspicion flickered in Lucy's eyelids as he stepped, slightly too quickly, through the doorway and out of her view. He closed the door behind him, exulting, but also fearing that she would discover his ruse. He sprang to the ladder and pulled himself up it and through the trapdoor as if escaping a monster that was groping for his legs. He emerged into a closet that was about the size of his room. He opened the closet into a lounge where a guest was lying on a sofa. Matthew ignored the guest's surprised face, and he walked out of the lounge as if nothing unusual was happening—then he ran.

9. They are still wearing the same clothing

Matthew ran through the hallways of the hotel, which were filled with guests costumed as birds. He was surprised so many of the guests were still awake. If he had been a guest instead of a manager, he would have been asleep and dreaming. But to sleep, he needed to find a suitable bed or sofa, where Lucy would never find him. He almost wanted to leave the hotel, as if leaving the hotel would by itself solve his troubles. But it was too late to hike through the woods to Greenburg, where his son was asleep in Aunt Demi's mansion.

He ran from lounge to lounge. All contained sofas, a few of which were hidden in corners. But a guest was in every lounge. Matthew wasn't yet prepared to lose the dignity required of a Hospitality Head by sleeping in view of a guest. He needed a place alone, where he could think, and not about what shouldn't have concerned him, such as kites or vomit, but about interesting subjects such as the relationship between geometric figures and their uses. He wanted, for example, to relate the frequency with which rectangles appeared in the Polka Dot Hotel to the frequency with which paragraphs appeared in stories such as the *Journey to the Lair of the Moon Golems*. But he had no time for such thoughts while looking for a suitable place to think them. He ran onward, and when he arrived at the balcony where he had been sleeping earlier that night, he found that the sofas had been retrieved from the field and repositioned in their proper places. They had probably been retrieved by the Infrastructure Manager. The hotel, apparently, functioned more efficiently than Matthew had believed.

He felt not only dispensable, but useless. If he had left through the woods that surrounded the hotel, nobody might have noticed his absence until somebody might have wanted to abscond with his office chair. If his contributions were useless, then he was nothing but the insignia that should have been emblazoned on his shirt. He had, however, been the Events Manager for only a day, and therefore shouldn't have been expected to perform adequately. But he had also attempted to retrieve the sofas in his regular capacity as the Hospitality Head.

He dropped on a sofa, as if never to rise from it. It was alongside the railing of the balcony, overlooking the field. Though it was unlikely to be the same sofa as that on which he had slept with Roselyn Spring nine years before, it was in the same position. To prepare for sleep, and remembering his deceased father, he began to pray, but as he was palming his hands together, a rustle disturbed him from the sofa beside him.

A young woman was lying on the sofa, and when she sat up, she said,

"I thought you might be here."

He wasn't prepared to speak with her, but he was relieved that she wasn't Lucy Crowe. She was costumed as a swan, and her hair was blonde. Despite his exhaustion, he habitually assumed the dignity of the Hospitality Head.

"You thought I might be here?" he asked.

"You always come here," said the young woman.

"Don't I know that?"

"Maybe you know me," said Matthew. "But maybe I don't know you."

"I'm Shellie Readling. Don't you recognize me?"

He lied and said he recognized her. The lie was appropriate because he had seen her the previous year at the spring festival, and therefore he should have recognized her, even though she had dyed her hair from light brown to bright blonde. He also should have recognized her because he had met her when she had been a child, and she had always considered him to be a special friend from her childhood, if not someone much more important than that. He was relieved that he didn't have to maintain the appearance of a Hospitality Head, but he wasn't pleased to see her, not only because he wanted to sleep, but because he wasn't prepared to talk to her about anything interesting. He hadn't expected to see her again. She had returned to college, at the age of twenty-five, to resume her studies toward becoming a polymer chemist. They had had a few interesting conversations about plastics and tinted glass, but they had usually talked about the *Dream of the Red Chamber* and the *Journey to the Lair of the Moon Golems*, both of which Shellie had read on his recommendation.

"Did you think I died?" asked Shellie.

"No," said Matthew, "but I wasn't expecting you."

"You didn't recognize me! Have you forgotten me?"

"No, but maybe I need to be alone now."

"Or some other reason, Matthew. Or should I call you Bill?"

"They know me as Matthew Matheson here."

"A new name for a new person?"

"A new name for someone who wants to be alone."

"You're alone too much, Matthew."

"Why? Think I'll become a monster?"

"I don't know. *Je ne sais pas!*—that's the only phrase I remember from French class."

"The monster in the *Journey to the Lair of the Moon Golems*," said Matthew. "Remember him?"

"The rosebud as tall as a man?"

"The rosebud that belonged to the woman. A few eyelashes were sticking out of it. And if you looked into the bud, you saw a human eye."

"And the eye was blinking, sometimes," said Shellie. "But mostly, it looked dead. I remember him."

"It was a scary story."

"But it's only a story, Matthew. You shouldn't hate everybody because of a story. There's always the exception."

"Such as you, for example?"

"Me?" asked Shellie, pushing aside her hair. "Me?— Me, I'm thinking of becoming a hermit!"

"You—a hermit? You came from Greenburg to join the spring festival. I never go to festivals, unless it's part of my job." He almost added that he had become the Events Manager, but his failure to retrieve the sofas reminded him of his uselessness. Furthermore, mentioning his new position might have seemed like bragging, or might have seemed that he was trying to attract her with his money, even though she would likely earn more than he would, if she were to become a polymer chemist, as everyone expected. But more importantly, Matthew had no desire to impress her because he didn't want her to be attracted to him. He wasn't attracted to her, though most would have considered her beautiful. He considered her beautiful, too, but her beauty interfered with the flow of his thoughts, which he found annoying.

"I want to be a hermit," said Shellie. "Didn't you tell me you wanted to be a hermit?"

"I probably said that," said Matthew.

"But now that you're a manager, you can't be a hermit."

"That's true."

"I'd like to be a manager, too."

"Why? Because I'm a manager?"

"Maybe," said Shellie. "Why not?"

"I'd rather be a hermit than a manager."

"It's good to be alone, Matthew. But it's better to be alone with somebody else. Do you ever feel that way?"

"No."

Shellie pushed aside her hair, and the wings of her swan costume flapped feebly. "But you have no one who can understand you!" she cried. "I'm the only one who can understand your language!"

"St Gemma Galgani told me that in a dream."

"I remember you talking about St Gemma," said Shellie. "I've been reading about her. They say she saw visions."

"She spoke to her angels, directly into their ears."

"That's how people should be for one another, Matthew. We become ourselves—through the other person. Don't you agree?"

Matthew said he agreed with her, but only because she was becoming aggravated by his responses, though her aggravation was hidden under a sweetly shy manner, which he had long discerned as a front for a very different person whom he saw only in flashes. She was, however, unaware that she was presenting herself as other than who she was—which made her performance especially convincing. Unlike Shellie, Matthew knew he was an actor, and he could therefore act somewhat like himself while talking to certain people, though he had never acted completely like himself because he feared to expose all of his ugliness even to a sympathetic person. But he had observed Shellie when she was with people whom she called her friends, and with each friend, she was different, and not merely a few degrees different, but diametrically different, as if at the other side of a rectangle, or even outside of it on a line that was connected to the tail of a flying swan. She was always presenting herself as others would have liked to see her, but for purposes of her own, which she had never revealed, and which she probably didn't even know herself, but which he could intuit as being, perhaps, threatening. He had therefore always been cautious around her, and had never told her anything beyond what he had considered safe.

10. Pretending to know

Matthew talked with Shellie all night. He eventually shifted the conversation to plastics and tinted glass, which were interesting subjects, at least to Matthew. Though he tried to end the conversation many times, he was grateful that she could tell him something about chemistry. During an interesting part of their conversation, when she seemed fully engaged, she sat beside him on his sofa. By morning, she was lying on him, asleep.

The triangular pines along the horizon were poking through a mist. Birds were crisscrossing the air, and chirping, hesitantly, as if unsure that the sun was still burning. Shellie was breathing on his face, and drool was dripping from her mouth. His arm was around her, not only because there was no other place to put it, but also because he wasn't opposed to embracing a shapely woman. Her skin was hot through the satin of her swan costume, but he was too exhausted to become aroused. Though he was determined to avoid being late for work, he wasn't able to stay awake until sunrise, despite a pestering thought about a man with a mustache whom Matthew almost expected to see somewhere nearby with a fiery candle.

When Matthew woke, it was late in the afternoon. Shellie had left. He had missed more than half a day of work.

The balcony had been opened for the customers of the adjoining restaurant. The Restaurant Head probably seen Matthew asleep, but might not have wanted to wake him. The Restaurant Head was a young man, and ambitious. He would have eagerly accepted a promotion to Matthew's position, regarding it as his rightful step in his ascension to be the Head Head.

As soon as Matthew was on his feet, he resumed, to the extent that he could, the appearance of a manager. He brushed his hair with his hands. He straightened his shirt and his pants. Despite his ordinary clothing, which lacked any insignia, guests usually distinguished him as a manager, probably because he had the air of knowing where others were and what they were doing, as if he were monitoring everything around him, and striving to conform reality to an ideal. He strode into the restaurant, which was full of people, though nobody was eating. He would have hesitated to walk among them if he had been acting as himself, but in the guise of the Hospitality Head, he strode confidently through the middle of them. He was crossing toward the exit, when the Restaurant Head, who had been hiding behind a partition, emerged like an actor who, after waiting impatiently for his cue, enters the stage to perform in a favorite scene.

Though only twenty-three, the Restaurant Head must have spent much of his life eating. He was so fat that he seemed unable to fit inside of himself. His cheeks overflowed into his chin. He was wearing a green suit with a red scarf that seemed to affix his head to his body.

"It's a serious situation!" said the Restaurant Head. "I'm surprised you survived it!"

Matthew pretended to know what the Restaurant Head had meant by "survived it." He conformed his face to match the seriousness that the discussion warranted.

"It's worse than anyone thought," said the Restaurant Head.

"It's a serious situation," said Matthew.

"It's a catastrophe!" said the Restaurant Head.

Matthew had often conversed on subjects about which he knew nothing. Such conversations, however, threatened to expose his incompetence. He had sometimes had to admit that he had misunderstood what the topic of a conversation was. In such situations, he would claim to have been referring to something else, which he had assumed his interlocutor to have understood, and the conversation would then appear to have been an understandable misunderstanding. But when referring to something as unusual as a catastrophe, it would have been difficult to claim that a different catastrophe had been his true subject. Though he had experienced a few personal events during the night that could have been characterized—though only by means of exaggeration—as catastrophes, such events should have been unknown to the Restaurant Head.

"Has anything like this happened before?" asked the Restaurant Head.

"Many times, many times," said Matthew. "Move aside, please. I must return to the office."

But the Restaurant Head didn't move aside, and Matthew had to retreat, which he despised doing before an inferior.

11. This may happen in a bedroom

As Matthew walked toward his office, he momentarily lost the appearance of a manager. He appeared uncertain of what he was and where he was going. He wished he were a moon golem. As a moon golem, he would have had an unquestionable purpose, which would have been designed in him at his construction, and he would have lived on the moon, where other moon golems would have helped him, even without having to ask for their help. His knowledge of a moon golem's characteristics wouldn't have been fruitlessly obtained from stories that most supposed were fictional, but would have been information necessary for his survival. But as he neared the office suite, he acted as if he were the Hospitality Head, in case any of the guests might identify him. His presentation, however, wasn't perfect, due to a brown spot on his shirtsleeve. He tried surreptitiously to wipe it off, but the spot had seeped into the fabric. It was probably a spot of Lucy's vomit. He decided to exchange the shirt for one he kept in his desk for emergencies, and he comforted himself with the thought that with only a single modification, he would appear not only exactly like a man, but like a manager, despite a night sleeping on a sofa.

A crowd was blocking the entrance to the office suite, but when Matthew announced himself as a manager, they parted for him, as if his arrival promised them deliverance from their problems. But after squeezing through them into the bright central room in the office suite, around which the individual offices were situated, he almost stopped breathing. Anxiety twitched his eyebrows. He pulled nervously at his stained shirtsleeve as he approached a woman who appeared to be someone he knew, but when she ignored him, he walked past her as if he were approaching someone else. The rectangular ceiling tiles suggested that there was more order in the room than he had yet perceived, and his stride became more assured. He had failed to maintain the dignity required of a Hospitality Head, however, and when Mr Plute called to him from a sofa along the wall, he desired more than anything to have remained asleep.

"Matthew Mathelson!" called Mr Plute, as if summoning him out of a crowd to humiliate him. "Come here! Sit beside me on this sofa!"

Mr Plute's fat body was stuffed inside a green shirt, which was probably the remnant of a parrot costume that he had worn the previous evening at the spring festival. His bald head seemed to have nothing on it except eyes. His skinny lips were almost invisible, and his nose was only a bump with a pimple on it. He was sitting on a sofa that was used by those waiting to see the Infrastructure

Manager, whose office was next to Matthew's. Mr Plute didn't ordinarily interfere with the hotel's operations, but when he exercised his power, he was decisive and surprising.

Matthew sat beside Mr Plute on the sofa, but as far from him as he could sit, pressing his leg against the sofa's arm, and leaning his head away. Though Matthew felt honored to have been invited to sit beside the owner of the hotel, he sensed that he was about to be condemned. But if his duties had been of no consequence, nobody would have been concerned that he was late. Matthew was in a peculiar position, however. His titles suggested that he was a man of consequence, but his actions had almost no impact on the hotel's operations.

"Matthew Mathelson," said Mr Plute, dropping his hand on Matthew's knee as if to push it through the floor, "you've been lost all morning."

"I'm sorry," said Matthew.

"Don't be sarcastic," said Mr Plute.

"I'm not being sarcastic. I'm sorry I wasn't here."

Mr Plute frowned as if a thought were snaking out of his eyes. "Is that what you're sorry about?" he asked, suspiciously.

Matthew admitted that there had been problems at the spring festival, but any problems had been inherent in the festival itself, and therefore couldn't be said to detract from it. Mr Plute rejected this contention. The spring festival had been a catastrophe. All of the guests had fallen ill! Excessive alcohol consumption may have been the cause of vomiting in individual cases, but rotten pears were the most probable culprit. Matthew listened as if he had already known everything Mr Plute was telling him.

"The Head Cook has been fired," said Mr Plute. "But you're responsible too. Have you heard the tale about the weirdy beardy man?"

"No," said Matthew.

"A long time ago," said Mr Plute, placing his hands on his fat belly as if preparing to push it into his legs, "a man had an only heir, a daughter. And in her bedroom, she had a box. She used the box to store her clothes. But one wintry day, she emptied the box. And she gave the empty box to the weirdy beardy man. Now the weirdy beardy man was afraid to open the box. He thought the box contained the daughter's hair, which represented her beauty. . . . But enough of that tale. It's best to be direct. I can say what you need to hear in two words. Do you want to hear them?"

"Maybe not," said Matthew, placing his arm across his chest to defend himself.

"You don't want to hear them. You want to live in the land of illusions. You've read the *Dream of the Red Chamber*, no?"

"Yes, I've read that, Mr Plute."

"Remember when Pao-yu dreams of the twelve beauties of Chinling?"

"Yes, in chapter five."

"Chapter five—somewhere around there," said Mr Plute, suspiciously. "How would you know exactly?"

"I remember things that interest me."

"That's your problem. Too much dreaming about Chinling."

"I've solved problems in my dreams," said Matthew. "Please don't smile as if what I'm saying can't be true."

"You should be compensated for sleeping? Is that what you're telling me?"

"Not for sleeping, Mr Plute. But for solving problems related to the hotel. That would be fair, Mr Plute. But I wouldn't request payment for dreams."

"But you're making that request now, aren't you?"

"No, Mr Plute. I only want to emphasize how much I'm thinking about the hotel, night and day."

"You're already being paid for that. If ideas come to you in dreams—good! But this is already included in your salary. There will be no extras for dreams!"

"Of course not, Mr Plute."

"It's as ridiculous as paying you for performance that's inadequate."

"I agree, Mr Plute. But this was my first day as the Events Manager."

"Are you telling me you're acceptably incompetent?"

"No, Mr Plute. But I might not be perfect on the first day."

"But if we paid you, you'd be paid for sleeping. Isn't that true?"

"Please consider my position. I'm only one person— but I'm extraordinarily committed."

"What's this about being an extraordinary person? You think you're extraordinary because you get ideas from dreams? Because you sleep on a sofa, in front of guests? Is this extraordinary?"

"No," said Matthew, barely able to speak.

"You're on probation," said Mr Plute. "One more mistake, and you're fired."

Matthew wanted to respond, but he had lost control of his eyebrow, which was twitching. He feared to lose completely the composure required of a manager. If he had shown himself as he actually was, his chances for promotion would have vanished. He had sought to portray himself as ambitious and conscientious. Perhaps he shouldn't have claimed to be an extraordinary person, even if his claim had been merely implicit. Nevertheless, to have presented himself as deficient would have doomed his chances for advancement irrevocably. His twitching eyebrow was merely one manifestation of the truth of his personality. His leg was also beginning to stiffen, which would aggravate his limp. When he stood, he revealed himself by the curve of his back as a man who was somewhat ridiculous.

12. This refers to what was said before

Matthew retreated to his office and closed its door. He sat at his desk. He had demolished the positive impression he had wanted Mr Plute to have of him. When he had accepted the position of Events Manager, in addition to his position as the Hospitality Head, he had mourned the loss of time that commitment to both of these positions required. The *Journey to the Lair of the Moon Golems* had been awaiting him on the pillow of his bed, before Lucy had discarded it somewhere in his room, probably on the floor, where it might have been covered with her vomit; but even if he would have found the book, he would have had no time to reread it and return to the glimmering groves of Bekanti. He noticed again the spot of Lucy's vomit on his shirtsleeve. It was a circular spot, the only circular object in his office, excepting his head. He opened the top left drawer in his desk and confirmed that it contained an extra shirt. The extra shirt was evidence of his competence. He wanted to show it to Mr Plute, but Mr Plute expected more than competence, as was only right.

Matthew wished to leave the Polka Dot Hotel and start anew as a manager somewhere else. He had attempted to quit his job before, but he had never found anyplace ready to hire him for the same remuneration. Few managerial positions were available, and most were filled as soon as they opened. Matthew had few connections at the hotel, and none outside of it. His options, therefore, were limited. But he enjoyed fantasizing about leaving for somewhere else, where he was sure to find the success that had eluded him. If those at the Polka Dot Hotel couldn't properly value his contributions, he would go where his contributions would be properly valued. But such aspirations were hopeless because he never intended to leave, despite all of his thinking about it. He merely wanted to believe that he had the option to leave, as if the option were sufficient to prevent him from committing himself entirely to the hotel. He wanted to preserve something of himself for himself, even if only as a possibility.

He looked at the wall, where he had often imagined the glimmering groves of Bekanti. A dried drip of paint reminded him of the roses as tall as trees, with honey dripping from their blooms. He longed to be outside of all boxes, all offices, like Befijop piping on his sylloma and stopping beneath a tree, in which a broken umbrella has been caught in the branches, wiggling in the breeze. If he could have lived in a story, he would have, but only as the hero. But being the hero might have required too much effort. He therefore would have been willing, maybe even might have preferred, to be a minor character in a long book, a character who appears now and then with something interesting to say, and then retreats to a quiet house where he plays a piano alone. He might have even preferred to be a character who was only mentioned in a book. His realization that he was willing to be insignificant inspired him to pray, but he stopped after a few words because he had said the words aloud. They might have been overheard by the Infrastructure Manager in the neighboring office, and the Infrastructure Manager might not have approved of prayers during the workday.

Matthew needed an assured solitude, perhaps even inside a box or rectube, not only to reread the *Journey to the Lair of the Moon Golems*, but to prepare for the day's work. The guests of the hotel had fallen ill. He wasn't prepared to respond to their complaints. He would almost certainly make mistakes while talking with so many people, and Mr Plute had warned him not to make even one mistake. He would have had to appear as a manager, which was the last thing he really was, and this required exertions beyond his capacity.

The longer he remained in his office, the more likely a

guest would come to issue a complaint about the festival, and once the complaints began, they would probably continue past the time to quit work. To prepare for such long hours, Matthew needed his proper sleep, which he hadn't obtained by sleeping on a sofa. He therefore decided to return to his room for a nap.

13. Does she always change her voice like that?

Matthew left his office and hurried through the crowded hallways toward his room. Whatever the situation, he appeared prepared to resolve it, as if he were bearing the powers of the hotel in his person. He regarded his intended nap as part of his duties. If he hadn't been at work, he would have been planning to sleep for nine hours, instead of nine minutes, but he nevertheless felt guilty, as if he were abandoning his duties instead of preparing for them more thoroughly. If he had been the Infrastructure Manager, maybe he could have performed excellently without sleep, but the Infrastructure Manager, though supposedly only one person, might have been delegating his duties to somebody else during the nights; otherwise, Matthew couldn't conceive how he could operate efficiently at all times.

Matthew required both sleep and dreams to sustain himself. Stories also sustained him. Even a single page from the *Journey to the Lair of the Moon Golems* sufficed to place him in a fictional place and time, where he walked the halls of the Mansion of Left Turns, where he could be other than whom he appeared to be when interacting with people who expected him to perform for them, as if he were on a stage. Even strangers expected him to present himself in a manner deemed appropriate. He was as if surrounded by an invisible rectube that extended an arm's length from his body. His rectube wasn't supposed to touch the rectubes that surrounded others. If his rectube touched another person's, he was expected to excuse himself, as if his presence were offensive. His gaze, likewise, was always pulling away from people. He was often scanning the walls.

The wallpaper in the hallways depicted parrots nesting in pear trees. Maybe the Infrastructure Manager had ordered the walls to be wallpapered with scenes appropriate for the spring festival. Or maybe the walls had always been wallpapered, and Matthew had never noticed them, though he had walked the same hallway for years. But on this occasion, he was noticing the wallpaper not because he had never seen it before, but because Shellie Readling had appeared in the hallway, and he had needed something that appeared to have drawn his attention from her. He pretended that he had been instructed to examine the wallpaper as part of his job, and therefore couldn't be disturbed, even to talk to a friend who was still somewhat distant, and who might yet vanish around a corner. He couldn't, however, find any irregularity in the wallpaper. The Infrastructure Manager had been typically thorough. Each rectangular sheet of the wallpaper had been aligned perfectly, never interrupting the flow of the scene, from parrot to identical parrot, like parents copying themselves in their children.

"You look as if you've seen a ghost!" cried Shellie, accosting him.

"Good to see you," said Matthew, pretending to be both surprised and pleased.

"Think I became invisible last night?"

"Why invisible?"

"Because you left me on the sofa."

"When?" asked Matthew, perplexed. "You were gone when I woke."

"You abandoned me! I was coming back."

"How was I supposed to know you were coming back?"

"By waiting for me. How else?"

Matthew hadn't had sufficient sleep to be prepared to contend with Shellie Readling and her astounding questions. He hadn't considered the possibility that she had planned to return to the sofa. Apparently, she had the fantastical belief that he was thinking about her more than he was. He had never said anything to her beyond a certain point, to prevent her from thinking he was attracted to her. Though many must have considered her beautiful, her beauty wasn't as interesting as the wallpaper. The beauty of the wallpaper could be discovered only after an examination. Shellie's beauty, like an annoying blinking light, required no effort to perceive. His attraction to her was too unthinking to engage him. Some men probably liked Shellie because of her appearance, but Matthew liked Shellie despite her appearance, though he liked her only as a friend, and not as a friend whom he actually knew, but only as a friend he was pretending to know. Not only was her hair always fixed in a different way, which made her almost unrecognizable to anyone who met her only once, but the expressions of her face seemed designed for her interlocutors. She was fascinating, but unknowable, like the inside of a drawer that contains something else every time it's opened.

"I understand," said Shellie. "You woke, I was gone. So I went to your room, thinking you were there. Your room was a mess! I cleaned it while waiting for you. You're welcome, by the way!"

Matthew knew, from conversational templates he had reviewed in novels, and also from his own experiences, that he was expected to thank Shellie for cleaning his room, but he was more annoyed by her intrusion than grateful for her help. He nevertheless avoided any show of annoyance, though he clenched his foot within his shoe.

"I cleaned the vomit off your blanket, too," said

Shellie, touching his arm.

Matthew flinched. She suddenly seemed like the *Laccifer lacca*. When the female of this species of insect is ready to lay its eggs, it attaches itself to a tree. After feeding on the sap, it secretes a resin in which it is eventually encapsulated, except for a few holes for its hairs to protrude and for its offspring to crawl out. A hair at the corner of Shellie's mouth reminded him of the likelihood that ugly surprises were lurking beneath her clothes, and the suddenness with which she had touched him startled him as much as finding a moth stuck on a spoonful of jelly that he was about to lick. Though he pretended his flinch hadn't expressed repulsion, he was unable to disguise his reaction completely, and Shellie, perhaps to test whether he was disgusted by her, touched his elbow again, and even squeezed it until he shook her away, though disguising the shake by reaching up to brush his hair with his hand.

14. This could have been different, too

Matthew told Shellie that he had to return to work, and he left her quickly; but he couldn't bear returning to his office, where he would have to confront the guests who were waiting to see him. When he was out of Shellie's sight, he considered circling back to arrive at his room from another direction, but if Shellie were to have encountered him during this maneuver, he would have had to explain where he was going, or would have had to admit that he had lied to her. She wasn't likely to consider "I must return to work" as equivalent to "I must return to my room to take a nap," though Matthew connected them because he couldn't work effectively without sufficient sleep. Nevertheless, he needed only a brief reprieve, perhaps only a few minutes, to regain the energy necessary to perform according to his expectations. He therefore entered a bathroom that was reserved for employees. He strode to the last stall in the row, entered it, pulled down his pants, and sat on the toilet. He would have shut his eyes, but he associated the reflections on the stall's luminous green door with the glimmering groves of Bekanti. He imagined an author lying on a bed while writing the story of Matthew Mathelson, and he remembered his son. He had long wished to write to him, but he had never been able to put the words together correctly. Every time he had begun to write what he had wanted to say, he would lunge in a new direction, fearing to lose the most important relationship in his life. Nevertheless, he tried again, writing on a notepad on which he recorded the complaints of the guests:

"Dear Adam," he wrote, "by the end of this paragraph you will have seen that I've anticipated the future. I can't say what I want to say because my words will be somewhat rectangular. I must proceed, therefore, by insinuation. After Turtledove left his father, he hid for a year in the Machine Forest, and when he came out again, his hat was still on his head, though he had become unrecognizable. Were I to finish this message, Adam, I might not deliver it to you. You might understand it to mean that you should turn left like everybody else, when it might be best to drop into a hole. Historians assume that human beings have never been flat, but the evidence from surviving paintings shows that human beings were flat until 1425, the year Masaccio painted *The Holy Trinity with the Virgin and St John*, which is the first surviving painting since ancient Pompeii to depict human beings as three dimensional. Remember, Adam, if you draw too many parrots, you'll believe they exist as you've imagined them. I'm glad your parrots aren't rectangular, but never assume a rectangular parrot is impossible."

Matthew looked at the wall of the bathroom stall, as if his next sentence may have moved there, but the wall showed nothing but the shadow of his head, which reminded him of his son's drawing of a parrot, a drawing which Matthew usually didn't notice because he had become accustomed to it being pasted at the upper left corner of a wall in his room.

He tried again, and for the last time, to write to his son. "Dear Adam," he wrote, "I'd rather tell you this in person, but we rarely see one another. I've come to see the pigeons as a symbol of your mother, though not a symbol that can be put into only one place like a piece that fits into a jigsaw puzzle, but a symbol that points in various directions toward the problems we've been having with management. As I tried to tell you in my previous message, the pigeons have entered the Mansion of Left Turns through a hole in the roof, and though management has ordered that they be evacuated, the Head Head has concluded that nothing more needs to be done, even though nothing has been done, which frustrates everybody who lives here except me; but I'm accustomed to disappointment. You'll see from this that I'm trying to say something to you, and to say it as gently as I can, which is causing me more difficulties than the pigeons are causing the Head Head. That was a joke, and if you're laughing, the joke wasn't successful because there should be nothing humorous about this message. My jokes are usually missed, however, so I encourage you to continue reading straight from here like an arrow, not like an arrow that descends parabolically due to gravity, as it actually descends in a vacuum, but you will please imagine this arrow to fly to the end of each line of text from left to right, in the same direction your eyes proceed when reading. You will understand me. I'm determined to be clear. There is a distance between people. This distance isn't only the distance that can be measured, but is a metaphorical distance, as if each of us inhabits a box. I'm living in a rectube that looks much like a closet and that serves as my room. The bed in my rectube is rectubical, and the picture you drew for me is rectangular, through no fault of your own, but due only to the convenience of using pre-cut paper, which usually is rectangular, a rectangle being the shape that many human beings prefer, as it is an efficient shape and familiar, too, because the human body is somewhat rectangular, excluding the head."

Matthew hadn't planned to mention any heads, but nevertheless, a head had entered his message. He saw no way to cut the mention of the head without falsifying what he wanted to say because a human body is approximately rectangular only if the head is disregarded, and therefore, the head had to be mentioned, if only to specify that it should be cut off. He was always looking for a reason not to send the message that he wanted to send to his son. He accepted any excuse whatsoever, whether legitimate or not. He was always telling himself that the message would make no difference, regardless of whether it was finished and delivered. He expected to be disappointed, but couldn't actually bear to be so. The hairbrush that Roselyn Spring had left in his room had caused him a similar dilemma. He could neither discard it nor keep it, but because he had to do one or the other, he had kept it, as this had preserved his option to discard it.

15. Or is pretending not to

Matthew was too exhausted to write another message to his son. He shut his eyes to imagine the groves of Bekanti more clearly, and he fell asleep. He had intended to sleep for no more than a few minutes; but when he woke, the lights were off in the bathroom, and the hotel was abnormally silent.

His absence had probably been noticed. The Head Head had probably been informed. Mr Plute might also have been notified. If so, Matthew's remaining years would be different than he had been expecting because he had been planning to rise to be the Head Head. But he had been absent before, without consequence, though never after having been warned not to make even a single mistake. He stood abruptly, but he couldn't leave the bathroom stall immediately because his legs were numb from sitting too long in the same position. While waiting for his legs to fill with blood, he lost his enthusiasm to return to an office that was almost certainly closed. He felt relieved. He had no further obligations, at least until the next day. He could therefore return to his room and read a few pages of the *Journey to the Lair of the Moon Golems*, and while pulling up his pants and exiting the stall, he imagined he was somewhere on the moon, in the darkness and silence. The bathroom could have been larger than the hotel, if his eyes could have been believed, because he could see nothing. He oriented himself in accordance with a configuration of the bathroom that may have existed only in his imagination, and he stepped toward where he believed the door would be and found it, even though he would have preferred to have found the groves of Bekanti.

He opened the door and walked quickly into the hallway, as if toward a goal, but his sleep hadn't refreshed him. His head felt detached from his body, as if he were pulling it behind him like a balloon of smoke from a kettle. After walking through many hallways, almost randomly, he decided to stop briefly at his office, to prove at least to himself that he was responsible, but when he entered the office, he felt like an intruder. The central room was dark except for a lamp next to the sofa where he had spoken with Mr Plute earlier that day. The sofa's seat cushion seemed to have been flattened, as if Mr Plute were still lying on it invisibly, or as if his weight had impressed the seat cushion permanently. Matthew didn't expect to meet him again, but noises were coming from one of the offices that surrounded the central room. When Matthew approached his office door, he was almost certain that the noises were coming from someone sitting at his desk. The noises stopped when Matthew stopped outside the door. He almost opened the door as if he were arriving for work, and he was prepared to act as surprised as he really was; but he paused. At the sound of a footstep, however, he feared that the intruder was coming to greet him, and not wanting to be found standing indecisively, he opened the door, almost expecting to see a ghost or an angel of death.

But the office was the same as it had been, with the same walls in the same positions, though maybe slightly expanded, though he couldn't be certain of this without measuring them. He had possibly opened the door to the wrong office. The man standing by the desk was one of Matthew's new assistants. Matthew had met him during the preparations for the spring festival, but he couldn't remember his name. He was about twenty years old, and he was smiling in the same way that he had been smiling when they had first met. Probably, the man smiled this same smile whenever he greeted anyone.

"Please don't be surprised, Matthew Mathelson," said the man.

Matthew mirrored the man's smile, which wasn't the smile Matthew usually used, and it felt odd, like a piece of food stuck to his chin. He hadn't expected to be addressed by name. Usually, before he went anywhere, he would prepare a list of topics, and also phrases and questions, so as to have pleasant interactions with those who might talk to him, but this time, being too preoccupied with his problems, and arriving at an office that he had expected would be empty, he had neglected to prepare for social intercourse. He remembered a few sentences from templates that he had prepared for other occasions, but neither "It's warm tonight" nor "I'm feeling better" seemed correct in the present context. Furthermore, he wasn't able to maintain the show of a calm demeanor because his eyebrows were twitching. At such moments, not uncommon in his life, he envied birds. Birds always knew what to sing, and they never had to prevent their eyebrows from twitching.

The man, however, wasn't noticing Matthew's twitching eyebrows, or he was pretending not to notice them. There are many friendly people who will try to put others at ease. Matthew seemed to have met one of them. The man introduced himself, but Matthew didn't attend to his name with sufficient concentration to remember it. The man continued talking about something or other, but Matthew wasn't listening to him because he was trying to recall the name that he had just heard. This had also happened to Befijop in the *Journey to the Lair of the Moon Golems*. Ever since Matthew had read that book, he had been experiencing much of what had happened in it. But if he allowed the man to speak too long, he would move outside the story, and wouldn't be able to use the excuse that Befijop had used in a similar situation.

"Excuse me," said Matthew. "Why are you here?"

"What don't you understand?" asked the man, in a deferential voice.

"Let's begin again. Your name?"

"Tom Burrows."

"You're one of my assistants?"

"I'm your Second Assistant."

"In my capacity as the Events Manager?"

"Yes, of course," said Tom Burrows, bewildered by the obviousness of what was being said.

Their conversation continued much like this:

. . . .?

. . . .

. . . .?

. . . ., ...?

. . . .

. . . . !

. . . ., ha ha ha.

Ha ha ha.

. . . .?

. . . . , ...

Matthew had often participated in such conversations. He knew what to say—until Tom mentioned Roselyn Spring.

"Did you say Roselyn Spring?" asked Matthew.

"She's here to see you. That's why I'm in your office. I was leaving you a note."

Matthew was too surprised to hide his surprise. The mention of Roselyn Spring seemed to prove that other people were influencing him in ways that couldn't be predicted. Did Tom Burrows also know about Matthew's son, Adam? He waited for Tom to provide further information, but when the wait became too prolonged to be comfortable, and when Tom's smile sprang back into his face, Matthew assumed that no more information would be volunteered. Maybe Roselyn had brought Adam, but hadn't told Tom. Or maybe Tom had seen the boy but hadn't known Matthew's relationship to him, and had therefore omitted this important detail. But whatever the reason for Tom's omission, Roselyn had come to visit, probably for purposes known only to herself. Perhaps she had come to visit Mr Plute, with whom she imagined she was in love, and from whom she was hoping to inherit the hotel. But if Mr Plute had been her sole objective, she wouldn't have visited Matthew's office. Matthew resented her intrusion. Why couldn't he have been left out of her imaginary life? He wanted his life to mirror a story that satisfied his wishes for success and honor. He wanted to be Befijop floating across the moon; but now he would have to be a wild-haired man, and Roselyn would call him Bill Robbins. He would have to appear to be somebody other than who he was; otherwise, Roselyn would cause problems that would be impossible to solve without exertions that were beyond what he could be expected to endure. It was exhausting to present himself in accordance with how he wished her to view him, but if he had acted solely in conformity with his own feelings, he would have been grossly self-indulgent, like an infant. The strain of having to perform in accordance with templates that were alien to his inclinations, however, required frequent reprieves. He often needed to be alone by a window, and any encounter with Roselyn Spring required a long period of preparation. He would have preferred to learn as much as possible about her visit, without seeming too curious about issues he wished not to disclose to an assistant, with whom his relations should have remained impersonal. He needed an indirect way to ask whether Roselyn had brought Adam, but before he could think of a way to inquire, Tom said,

"Not to be personal—but should I tell you what's being said about you?"

"What's being said about me?" asked Matthew.

"I can't say. Or—I shouldn't say. Is that enough for you to know what it is?"

"What are you talking about?"

"Don't ask me to explain. But they're talking about you at the office."

"What are they saying?"

"They're talking about your hair," said Tom. "Please don't be offended. You don't comb your hair—that's what they're saying."

"I don't always remember to comb my hair," said Matthew.

"Please forget I said it," said Tom. "I thought I could talk to you—really talk to you. But I'm young. I shouldn't have said anything."

Matthew suspected that a rumor about his poor performance during the spring festival had spread through the office, but to avoid the impression that this rumor was true, Matthew showed no hint that Tom's hint had been understood. To have shown any concern whatsoever about what Tom had implied would have confirmed even the worst rumors, which were probably beyond what could be expected even in fictions such as *Alice in Wonderland*. Furthermore, if anything had been said about the wildness of Matthew's hair, he would have been foolish to comb it, as this would suggest that he was easily influenced by what others said about him. His position was too important to worry about the positions of each of the strands of his hair, as if these strands could be positioned permanently throughout the day, without being blown awry by a closing door or cough. He desired to perform perfectly, but if perfection extended even to the positioning of each of his hairs, he would have had to comb his hairs too frequently. Nevertheless, he conceded that he ought to adjust his appearance to the expectations of his boss, and he was willing to comb his hairs even as often as once a week, but only if this change would seem to be unrelated to what his subordinates were saying about him.

Though Matthew considered himself to be as logical as a moon golem, he was easily distracted. If he had been able to concentrate on only one question at a time, he might have solved at least one of his difficulties, at least provisionally and approximately, if not to his satisfaction. He wanted to be certain, but certainty appeared beyond the capacity of his mind, which suggested that he was a human being because the moon golems had been designed to accept certain axioms. And yet, he wasn't certain that he was certain of nothing. How could he be certain that he was certain of nothing if there was nothing about which he could be certain? Sometimes he believed he certainly had a head, for example, and yet, when he wasn't thinking about his head, it seemed possible it didn't exist, just as the existence of his foot became questionable as soon as it was hidden in his shoe. Of course, he wasn't truly worried about whether he had a head, or whether he was a man, or whether he should comb his hair, but he was worrying about these things to avoid thinking about Roselyn's visit.

He was often worrying about things that he didn't know anything about, and he was often awake late at night, sometimes even until morning. He suspected that his sleeping patterns were related to the periods of the moon, but to test this hypothesis he would have had to remove the moon, which was impractical. Practicality, therefore, determined the limits of what could be shown by experiment. This was disappointing because Matthew had many questions that were impractical to test. But "the room had one window," which was a famous quote from the *Journey to the Lair of the Moon Golems*, raised no such impracticalities. It was easily confirmed that Matthew's room had only one window. He couldn't always see this window at night, however, probably because it was curtained. But even if experiments couldn't be performed to address all questions, there may have been other methods for obtaining apparently reliable information, such as prayer. He doubted his prayers would be answered, however, because he hadn't been able to pray as charitably as St Gemma Galgani.

16. To escape without seeming to

Matthew was determined to end the conversation with Tom Burrows as quickly as possible, but without providing his subordinate any hint that anything was amiss. If he had suggested that the announcement of Roselyn Spring's visit was like the unexpected delivery of a kite, he would have inspired more rumors about his activities. But Tom seemed to expect to hear something about Roselyn Spring, or at least his smile seemed to be expecting to become more friendly with Matthew, probably on the assumption that Matthew would promote those whom he liked. But Matthew wasn't the kind of manager who rewarded the admiration of his subordinates. He recommended promotion only on the basis of merit, or at least he believed he recommended in accordance with this ideal; and even if he sometimes failed to be objective, he resented Tom's implication that he could be swayed by a persistent smile, which was becoming annoying, mostly because of its sameness.

"You seem friendly," said Matthew. "It's good to seem friendly when dealing with guests at the hotel."

In response to this praise, Tom's smile expanded almost beyond the boundary of his face, and Matthew, believing that a suitable ending to their conversation had been reached, turned, almost too abruptly, and left the office, but without a sense of relief. Though he had escaped without damaging his supervisory authority, he hadn't handled the situation as well as he would have liked, nor had he been prepared for difficulties that should have been foreseeable.

But as he walked the hallways, he wasn't acting like a manager. He was acting as if he were Bill Robbins. He pretended he was taller. He pretended he was dangerous. He had to pretend to be Bill Robbins because Roselyn wouldn't have accepted him as he really was. He had no influence over her unless he appeared to be at least a robber, if not worse. But Matthew wasn't accustomed to being Bill Robbins while at the Polka Dot Hotel, and he felt as if he had become one of the guests. His role had changed, like an actor who plays two parts but never confuses them, though playing one after the other. As Bill, he walked as if wading through sand, and his limp seemed the result of an injury acquired in a fight. Matthew, as the Hospitality Head, would have regarded Bill as a potential disturbance, to be monitored, and to be removed from the hotel at the first infraction; and Bill would have regarded Matthew as a sycophant, to be pitied for his conformity to the standards of those who had money.

He shuffled through the hotel, up stairs and down stairs, and into green rooms filled with clocks and stuffed parrots. He was intending to ascend to the hole in the roof through which pigeons were infiltrating the hotel, so he could lie more plausibly about having inspected the hole during his absence that afternoon, but he was noticing that every wall was rectangular. Most walls were rectangular. Nothing, therefore, was odd about the shape of the walls in the Mansion of Left Turns, but it was odd that Matthew had noticed what he had always seen. With a quiver of surprise, he noticed that the doors were also rectangular! Had the shape of the walls been inspired by the shape of the doors? And had the shape of the doors been inspired by the shape of the human body? The human body was approximately rectangular, except for the head. It was therefore probable that doors had been designed to accommodate human beings. After passing through many doorways, all of which were rectangular, Matthew arrived at the balcony where the sofas were. He hadn't been planning to lie on the sofa again, where he had lain with Roselyn Spring, but as soon as it was before him, he lay on it, as if it had been awaiting him.

The moonless night seemed symbolic of his absence of illusions. He imagined he was invisible in the darkness. He needed solitude to consider the implications of Roselyn's visit. She had probably come to demand more money for their son, even though Matthew was giving more than he could afford. His inability to provide was of no importance when measured against her enormous desires. He dreaded returning to his room, where she would probably be awaiting him. He needed to be alone, where he could read a scary story, and forget the trivial problems that were requiring too much of his limited time on Earth. But his solitude was interrupted by a laugh from the sofa beside his. He feared that the man with a mustache was coming to tell him of yet another ghost, but instead, Shellie Readling, with a rose braided in her blonde hair, was reddening with pleasure because of the success of her trick.

"Yes—it's me," she said, giggling.

"Shellie!" cried Matthew, as stunned as he really was. "You're here? Again?"

"I wanted to show you something. Remember?"

"You've been waiting for me here?"

"Of course not, Matthew. Don't be silly!"

Matthew had never seen her so mischievous; he therefore felt comfortable presenting himself as other than whom she might have expected. He pulled himself into a sitting position. His preparations to meet Roselyn Spring had injected elements of Bill Robbins into his presentation. If he had cancelled these elements upon Shellie's appearance, the fakery of his presentation would have been evident. But perhaps she was too preoccupied with herself to notice anything different about him. Maybe her self-centeredness was different than his. His self-centeredness—though excessive—was excusable because it was partly a reaction to other people, so as to interact with them successfully. But Shellie's self-centeredness may have disregarded the expectations of other people entirely. Or maybe Shellie couldn't perceive elements of Matthew Mathelson that were inconsistent with her conception of him. Or maybe he wasn't acting as much like Bill Robbins as he believed. He may have only been imagining that he was presenting himself as a dangerous man, when he was actually only showing himself to be pitiable.

"You abandoned me last night," said Shellie.

"I woke—you weren't here," said Matthew. "We talked about this before."

"We did. But I'm reminding you. Remember? I rearranged your room! I'm waiting for you to compliment me."

Instead of responding, Matthew considered whether he wanted to sleep with her because "I'm waiting for you to compliment me" was obviously an invitation to prove himself eligible for that opportunity. He would become ineligible if he complimented her because if Shellie could obtain her desires merely by means of a request, no further enticement would be necessary, and the absence of any ensuing drama would make him as boring as other men. She wouldn't have troubled herself to wait for him on the sofa only to receive a compliment as soon as she asked for one. She had other expectations, which suggested that Matthew may have been acting somewhat like a seductive Bill Robbins, instead of an evasive Matthew Mathelson. Or maybe his different presentations of fictitious selves had been joined by Shellie into one impression, such as shyness or aloofness or arrogance, depending on her preference. It's a convention to foreshadow a surprise, so as to make it appear to be a natural consequence, and therefore believable to a reader who, nevertheless, has experienced many surprises in reality without requiring any foreshadowing to believe they happen. But if a pigeon were now to fly over their heads, the narrative would be interrupted like the graph of a function that has a point outside the curve at $x=28$. A similar discontinuity occurred within Matthew because, to his surprise, he knew not only that he didn't want to sleep with Shellie Readling, but that he didn't want to sleep with anybody ever again, not only to avoid the consequences, but to obtain a solitude where he could develop into somebody he could barely remember, but who seemed to have been placed in a drawer that he would recognize if it contained the original items that had been placed within it.

"You probably rearranged my room because you were bored," said Matthew.

"You should still compliment me for it," said Shellie.

"I shouldn't. And there's something else I shouldn't do."

"I'll leave, if you're angry."

"Do I look angry?" asked Matthew.

"Maybe you're hiding it."

"Maybe I am."

"Do you want me to leave?" asked Shellie, surprised.

"If you want to leave, you can."

"I have other things to do—but I didn't mean to suggest anything."

Matthew realized not only that Shellie wouldn't leave willingly, but that she planned to sleep with him, probably for more than one night, and maybe indefinitely. She had probably tidied his room to learn what she could about him, especially about his financial situation. Whatever she had found, she had apparently been sufficiently pleased. She had probably been waiting for him at least an hour. Lying on her sofa was a book—*Persephone's Rose*—which she had been reading. Atop the book was a damp, crumpled tissue. Shellie had wiped her nose with it. The tissue seemed to foreshadow a gradual accumulation of her possessions in his room. Before her occupancy would become established, he had to escape, without seeming to escape; otherwise, there would be the usual difficulties. He therefore proposed that instead of sleeping again on the sofa, they drink a bottle of wine together. He insinuated that something "more interesting" would happen if they drank a bottle of wine. He immediately regretted this insinuation, and wished he had thought of something more appropriate.

"I don't drink alcohol," said Shellie. "But I'll make an exception. Should we drink here, or in your room?"

She was obviously suggesting that they return to his room, which would involve Matthew in difficulties from which he would never escape. He still had a chance to live alone, if only he could keep Shellie on the balcony, a neutral territory where he could leave without closing a door. But he had proposed the bottle of wine, and therefore had implicitly offered to provide it. But he was unwilling to buy anything for her, not only because the purchase would suggest that he was compensating her for favors that he would later receive, but also because he disliked buying anything that he didn't want. But because the purchase of a bottle of wine was far less expensive than the costs of allowing her into his room, and because the purchase compensated her for the work she had expended in attempting to charm him, and was therefore not his worst option because it might satisfy her, at least temporarily, he proposed that he buy a bottle at the adjoining restaurant, if it was still open—which he hoped it wasn't. He was about to ask what kind of wine she preferred when she turned with a squeal of delight to greet a young woman whom she seemed to know intimately.

This young woman was Lucy Crowe. This itself was surprising, but the intimacy between Shellie and Lucy was more surprising yet, perhaps as surprising as Lagrange's theorem, which provides that every natural number is expressible as the sum of four or fewer perfect squares. Matthew's knowledge of Lagrange's theorem, and of other theorems just as surprising, allowed him to accept surprises as if he had been expecting them, and he therefore greeted Lucy while maintaining his composure.

"Hello, Matthew," said Lucy, adjusting her black hat. "Do you know Shellie?"

"Yes, I know Shellie," said Matthew. "And you know I know Shellie. You and Shellie have probably been talking about me all day!"

"Is that what you think?" asked Lucy, and she laughed as if her laugh had been scheduled yesterday for this precise moment.

"Yes, that's what I think—and I have other thoughts, too," said Matthew.

"But how should I know you know her?" asked Lucy. "You and I are strangers!"

"That's true," said Matthew.

"You're upsetting me," said Lucy.

"I hope you're not feeling sick again!"

"When was I ever sick? You must be talking about somebody else."

"I'm talking about the Twelve Girls with the Golden Hairpins," said Matthew. "I dreamed that each of them was sleeping in a drawer. They all ended the same way. That's from the *Dream of the Red Chamber*."

Matthew realized that he sounded incoherent, but both Lucy and Shellie seemed to have understood him, which probably indicated that they had stopped listening. Or maybe they didn't care whether they had understood him, but wanted only for him to believe that he had been understood, which was sufficient for their purposes. But regardless, their lack of concern for him was evident. He could say anything he wanted, and they would look at him with the same empty expressions, which were ready to be filled with whatever would appear to be most apt. He wished, however, to remain inside the boundaries of a typical conversation, where everything would be more predictable. But before he could shift the conversation to the weather, Shellie said to Lucy,

"This is Matthew. He's a friend."

Matthew was surprised that Shellie had called him a friend because it had seemed—just a minute ago—that she had desired to sleep with him. He wasn't, however, as relieved as he would have expected. He had enjoyed imagining that she desired him. He suddenly suspected that he knew himself quite well because he could argue with his feelings and declare them absurd. His situation was much improved now that Shellie had called him a friend because he needed only to agree with her to delay the joining of themselves on either a bed or a sofa. But he was nevertheless disappointed. Many men would have liked to sleep with Shellie, though only because of her beauty, and not because she sometimes seemed to be an interesting person. Maybe she actually was an interesting person. Maybe he had made a mistake by resisting her too much. In a few years, her beauty would diminish, or even vanish, after which they might have pleasantly discussed polymers in a lit room, without distractions.

"I first met Shellie when she was a child," said Matthew. "She's always been a friend."

"I don't like this," said Lucy. "We might as well be strangers! What's happened to us?"

"Us?" asked Matthew.

"I won't hide it anymore!" cried Lucy.

"Have you noticed that there's no moon tonight? Maybe it will rain," said Matthew.

"I won't hide it," said Lucy, "and you won't, either! Do you think this is a game?"

"Let's talk about the weather," said Matthew.

"You think this is a game? After what you did to me? After what you did to me!"

Matthew wanted to defend himself, but defending himself would have only convinced her that he knew she could hurt him, possibly grievously. By failing to respond, he was suggesting that no defense was necessary because nobody would believe her accusation. But she might interpret his silence as evidence that he feared her, or as an invitation to continue her attack. She was pulling at her hat while looking at him from the side, as if he wasn't worthy of her attention. If he could remain insignificant, she might decide that a victory over him would add nothing to her status, or would even diminish it. But if she already esteemed him—perhaps due to Shellie's influence—he would have to humiliate himself, maybe even by falling at her feet to confess that he loved her, which would repulse her, like receiving the adoration of a worm that has been feeding on a corpse. But he would have to fall at her feet without sarcasm, which would be difficult, and maybe beyond his capacities. Or he could lie and say she was beautiful, which would be especially complimentary because she was in the vicinity of the truly beautiful Shellie Readling. But again, he would have to compliment her without sarcasm, though she would ignore any hint that he wasn't being honest, if only to accept the compliment within Shellie's hearing. But whatever he decided to do, he had to change her feelings toward him, else her attacks would likely continue, even until his destruction.

"Lucy," he said, "you're impossible to understand! You're beautiful—but not too beautiful! I wish you'd leave!"

Matthew was prepared to elaborate along these lines, but with every word he was in danger of annoying her, or of even canceling any good feeling he might have succeeded in creating; and so, as soon as her face softened—and even acquired an attractive flush—he stopped, as if overwhelmed by what he was saying, and the blush of embarrassment that spread from his forehead to his neck was such an apt accompaniment to his outburst that both Lucy and Shellie sucked in a breath. Lucy probably believed his outburst was meant for her because he had addressed her by name, but Shellie seemed to believe that he was actually addressing her, as if he could only express his secret feelings for her by pretending to address them to someone else.

17. Not this! Not this!

Even if Matthew had had more to say, he would have remained as silent as he resolved now to be, while sitting on the sofa and staring down from the balcony at the rectangular patches of light that stretched across the field from the hotel's windows. Neither Lucy nor Shellie seemed interested in engaging with him further. Perhaps they sensed that he would say nothing more flattering than what he had said, and therefore would have only dispelled the pleasant afterglow of his compliment if he had said anything more. They were soon sitting beside one another on the adjoining sofa and talking to one another. Each of them appeared to have a hidden goal toward which each was meandering, around the meanderings of the other. But Matthew wasn't interested in what they were saying, until Lucy said,

"He doesn't know we're talking about him!"

"I don't care if you talk about me," answered Matthew, appearing as unconcerned as he desired actually to be.

"Don't be offended," said Lucy.

"Why assume I'm offended?" asked Matthew.

"Don't be silly," said Shellie. "I'd be offended, too, if I'd heard something like that about me!"

Matthew assumed that their criticism of him had been severe, even though they were teasing him as though what they had said was insignificant, or as though they expected him to disregard their words. Maybe—he flattered himself—they admired him too much to expect he could be influenced by them. But though Shellie and Lucy had seemed to consider him worthy of their romantic interest, they probably regarded him as nothing more than a handsome figure, or as a tool that it would be worthwhile to obtain, so as to elevate themselves in the envies of other women. But this assumed they were romantically interested in him, or were at least tolerating him for various purposes; and for these purposes, Shellie and Lucy might have assumed that either of them could have acquired Matthew when needed, with no more effort than that required to show their legs.

"I want to know what he's thinking," said Lucy.

"I was thinking I should leave," said Matthew. "Then you can say what you really think about me."

"We wouldn't talk about you," said Lucy. "You're not important enough."

But wasn't Matthew Mathelson important? He believed he was important. He thought about himself almost exclusively. It seemed right, therefore, that others should discuss him, if only to criticize him, if only to say something cruel. To talk about another person at least acknowledges that person, if only as a tool or decoration. And even if the talk was aimed only at gathering information so as to better manipulate somebody, it nevertheless signified that the somebody was significant, if only to be used and discarded.

"I'm leaving," said Matthew, "but I'll come back. I'll bring you a bottle of wine."

He stood from the sofa and strode into the adjoining restaurant. He had left too abruptly for either Lucy or Shellie to call him back, which they probably wouldn't have wanted to do. He probably could have left without announcing that he was leaving, but the announcement prevented him from being stopped because neither Lucy nor Shellie were likely to object to receiving a bottle of wine in exchange for nothing. But despite his announcement, he had no intention of buying anything for them, and when he passed through the restaurant and entered the hallway, he believed he had escaped.

He couldn't return to his room because Roselyn was probably checking it periodically, if she wasn't already living in it. She wouldn't have visited the Mansion of Left Turns without visiting him, at least once, if only to torment him. He needed to find another place to sleep, if only for a night or two. He rejected sleeping on one of the sofas in one of the many lounges throughout the hotel because he would have probably been found by a guest and reported to the Infrastructure Manager. His best option was to sleep in an empty room, maybe even the room where the pigeons had infiltrated the hotel through a hole in the roof. But as he was ascending a staircase, Shellie ran up behind him and accosted him.

"I knew you weren't coming back," she said.

"Do you know what's happened?" asked Matthew. He was whispering as if about to tell a secret.

"You need to tell me," said Shellie.

"Remember Roselyn Spring?"

"Is she here, too?"

"She can't see me with you. Understand?"

"That's why you've been acting like this!"

Matthew didn't correct her. Her conclusion was not only convenient for him, but convincing to her. She understood all of his difficulties; she forgave him for anything he might have done. He had told her about Roselyn before, many times. She was familiar with all of his stories. He hadn't planned to use Roselyn as an excuse to be alone, and yet the result couldn't have been better because Shellie not only understood him but commiserated with him. He was almost proud of the effectiveness of his excuse until Shellie grabbed his arm.

"Come with me!" she cried, and she dragged him from the staircase into a hallway.

He followed her, but only because she had surprised him just when he had believed himself safe.

"Where are we going?" he asked.

"Here!" she cried. "This window!"

It was an ordinary rectangular window, but they were higher in the tower than Matthew had expected. When he looked down through the window, he felt as if the ground, far below, had smacked his face. He looked away, dizzy, but when he looked again at Shellie, he realized she hadn't looked out the window even once, but was looking at him, as if examining something under a microscope. Her eyebrows, which she had dyed and plucked, were twitching. She seemed to have transformed into a person he had never known.

"What's special about this window?" asked Matthew.

"It's like a story in a book!" cried Shellie. "Do you know what happens next?"

Matthew realized that nothing had happened as he had planned. He was in more difficulties than he could have imagined that morning. How had everything changed so quickly? Or maybe everything had always been as it was, and he was only recognizing it now, in one overwhelming realization. He had never planned, had never even considered what was about to happen. But when Shellie sprang to her tiptoes and flung her arms around his neck, the nearness of her pretty face, which was almost circular, was demanding one response. She had probably been planning this moment since the previous spring festival. But regardless of when she had chosen him for this role, he was on her stage, under her lights. He reached his hand around her, though only to steady himself as a result of her sudden embrace. The corrugated back of her dress was damp with sweat. His mind sprang into the sky. He kissed her as softly as possible, and he held the kiss for as long as it takes to swallow a bite of cake.

18. Sufficiently to be convincing

While kissing Shellie, Matthew acted as though he had been fashioned according to Shellie's desires. He wanted to kiss her as she would have liked to have been kissed because he wanted to think of himself as being good in bed, but he didn't want to please her so much that she would desire they kiss again. He planned to act as though they had only reenacted a scene from a book. He planned to laugh as soon as the kiss was over, as if to say that it could have meant nothing to her, but as he was pulling away, a whiff of her astringent shampoo caught in his nostril, and before he realized what was about to happen, he sneezed through her hair, and almost on her face. He wasn't embarrassed. He couldn't feel penitent for what had only been a physical reaction, though he knew it was objectionable to sneeze on other people.

"You sneezed in my hair!" cried Shellie.

Matthew would have apologized, in accordance with the typical conversational templates for such situations, but instead of being annoyed by the sneeze, Shellie seemed ready to accept him sneezing on her again, if that was what he would have liked.

"You understand what I have to do," said Matthew.

"I do—or I don't," she said. "One of those?"

She seemed to be asking whether or not she was interpreting him correctly. Maybe his face wasn't congruent with his words. But he sensed that she didn't want an explanation that was even partially true, especially not after their kiss, which she had been expecting possibly for a year. But before he could extricate himself from the situation with a lie, she promised to help him in any way she could, and while he was explaining why he couldn't accompany her, she put her arm into his and led him to a newly constructed area of the hotel. Though Matthew was the Hospitality Head, he had never visited this area, which was reserved for the best guests, who were served by an elite department. He wasn't allowed to enter the area without authorization from Mr Plute, or at least from the Head Head, who would have likely disapproved of his presence there. But before Matthew could convince Shellie that they shouldn't enter an area reserved for the best guests, she pulled him into a room, as if he had to enter it before anyone would see them together.

"These are my rooms!" she announced. "My suite of rooms!"

"This is where you're staying?" asked Matthew, incredulously.

They were standing in a lounge, adjacent to a kitchen and dining room, with a closed door that probably opened to the bedroom. Shellie seemed to have been living there for many months. She had certainly made herself at home. Without seeming to examine everything, Matthew glanced at the tall walls, illuminated only by a small lamp. A pile of laundry filled a corner of the room; a bra was hanging from a painting to dry.

"How can you afford this place?" asked Matthew.

"I can't," said Shellie.

"Then how are you living here?"

"I'm supposed to pay, but I can't. What can they do? They can't get money from me if I don't have any!"

"I'm sure something will happen to you," said Matthew.

"I'm not worried. Somebody will pay for it."

She invited him to sit on the sofa. It was a large sofa, but it was filled with so many pillows that there was no place for anyone to sit. Matthew made a place for himself by pushing aside the pillows, and he sat, uncomfortably, in the place that he had made, with pillows pressing against him from all sides.

"Would you like something to drink?" Shellie asked. "A beer?"

It was odd that she was offering him a beer because she supposedly never drank alcohol, except on special occasions, but Matthew pretended not to have noticed the inconsistency. She probably had a good explanation—or could think of one—and he wasn't curious enough to uncover every mystery, especially not if the inquiry would delay his escape.

"Yes, thank you," said Matthew. "A beer—and then, I must leave."

"I know," said Shellie, as if she had never expected him to stay longer than a minute. "I'll get the beer later. First, I want to light a candle!"

But instead of lighting a candle, she opened a book and handed it to him. The book had probably been bought at a gift shop. It was the kind of book that lovers give to one another to express the standard feelings that are expected on occasions such as birthdays. The page that she had opened for him was bordered with hearts. In the center was a poem:

> The gooseberries grow on an angry tree,
> And little Melinda will pick one for me,
> She'll prick her finger, one two three,
> She'll rip her skirt, and bloody her knee.
> The gooseberries grow on an angry tree.

"It's my favorite poem," said Shellie. "But I shouldn't have shown it to you."

"Why not?" asked Matthew.

"Because you're not reacting as I hoped."

"How should I react?"

"You should know—without having to be told. Wait! I forgot the candle!"

She hurried to a cabinet and opened its drawers, looking into each and pulling out candle after candle, rejecting each of them with comments such as "too pointy" or "too melted," until finally, after reviewing the merits of more than fifty, she selected a big, lopsided candle and lit it. She carried this candle almost reverently to Matthew, holding it out for him to take, but when he made no move to take it, she placed it beside him on the armrest of the sofa, where it balanced precariously.

"Why the candle?" asked Matthew.

"I don't understand you," said Shellie. "This is disappointing."

"I feel as though I don't know you suddenly."

"I've known you since I was a child, Matthew."

"But you've changed—since a minute ago."

"I'm only trying to understand you, Matthew."

He didn't want her to understand him too well. He doubted she would have liked him if she had known him as he was, and even if she would have liked him as he was, he wouldn't have trusted her with that knowledge, which could be used to manipulate him, or to avenge herself should he fail to act according to her desires. Furthermore, she would better enjoy falling in love with him if she fell in love with him as she imagined him to be. But Matthew didn't want her to fall in love with him, even if she would only fall in love with an illusion to which he was attached. He wanted to present himself as someone she could neither love nor hate, which meant he would have to pretend to be yet another person.

"Shellie," he said, "don't try to know me. I'd disappoint you."

"But I already know you," said Shellie. "And you're not disappointing me. You need to be happy about that."

"What I need is a place to sleep. I can't go back to my room tonight."

"I know. That's why you're here, Matthew, with me."

He considered sleeping on her sofa, but only if he could sleep on it alone, and only if he could wake early in the morning and leave without waking her. He wanted to arrive at the office before anyone else, to show Mr Plute, and to show himself, that he was competent enough to be both a Hospitality Head and an Events Manager. But staying in her room would be a risk that he wasn't certain he could accept, even if it would prevent the difficulties that were likely to occur should he encounter Roselyn Spring before he was prepared.

"May I sleep here—just for tonight? On this sofa?" asked Matthew.

"Yes," said Shellie. "I'm inviting you to stay!"

"Then I'll stay. I'll be leaving tomorrow, early. Thank you."

He took off his shoes, expecting that she would leave him so he could prepare for a good night's rest. But she seemed to be expecting him to say something that he had obviously forgotten. He believed, however, that he had said everything necessary, and that saying anything more would result in a new problem that he wasn't prepared to handle. He was relieved when she said nothing in response to his silence. She was facing the wall, but without seeming to look at it. Then, as if having received a feeling that required a response, she left through the door into her bedroom, without looking back at him. As soon as she was gone, Matthew assumed that though she might have been annoyed, she had accepted that they wouldn't be doing anything that she might have expected to follow their kiss. But after unbuttoning his shirt, and as he was lying on the sofa, Shellie returned, her face twisted with rage.

19. It happened, now explain it

Matthew was unprepared to respond to Shellie Readling's rage, especially when he was anticipating an enjoyable sleep alone on her sofa while listening to the raindrops that had begun to splash against the window. But as soon as he saw her face, which was purpling due to her lack of breathing, he knew he wouldn't escape being punished. He shouldn't have accepted her invitation to sleep in her room, not even alone on her sofa, where he had foolishly believed himself safe. The kiss had obviously disappointed her, but she wasn't shouting about the kiss. Instead, she was shouting about wrongs that he had done to her many years ago. He was almost certain that a few of her accusations had involved another man, unless her version of what had happened differed so much from his that the two versions almost couldn't be seen as referring to the same event. Her accusations, however, provided him with the lucky opportunity to declare himself unworthy of her. He decided to leave immediately for another sleeping accommodation, but before he could grab his shoes, a man called from Shellie's bedroom:

"Who's that? Is that you?—Shellie?"

"Yes, William," answered Shellie, sweetly. "It's me!"

"Who's William?" asked Matthew.

"It's William Williams!" said Shellie.

A man appeared at the doorway of the bedroom. He was naked except for a blanket that he had pulled off the bed and wrapped around his waist. He wasn't, however, named "William Williams," unless he had forgotten his name since earlier that evening and had assumed a new name merely to avoid the embarrassment of having forgotten his true one. Or maybe he had another, more sensible reason to have called himself by another name. Or maybe he had chosen "William Williams" for its memorable and pleasing alliteration. His actual name, however, should have been sufficiently pleasing, unless it was also fictitious. Indeed, "Tom Burrows" should have been adequate for most purposes. But when Tom saw his boss sitting on the sofa, he showed only a twitch of surprise, followed by a smile that seemed to know what had happened.

"This is William Williams," said Shellie, her smile mirroring Tom's. "William is the nephew of Mr Plute, the owner of the hotel."

"This is interesting," said Matthew.

"My friends call me *William*," said Tom.

"I didn't expect to see you here," said Matthew.

"Do you know him?" asked Shellie.

"I've known him—for a few days," said Matthew. "And this is his room?"

"Yes—it's the best room in the hotel," said Tom.

"You don't seem embarrassed by that," said Matthew.

"Why should he be embarrassed?" asked Shellie. "Mr Plute lives in an even better room in the tower."

"Have you visited that, too?" asked Matthew.

"William has promised to introduce us."

"This is interesting," said Matthew.

"Is it really very interesting?" asked Tom, and he shifted his weight to his other foot, which was the first clue that he was more anxious than he was showing himself to be. Matthew was amazed by Tom's acting abilities. The man was almost the perfect facade. He smiled as easily as shifting a ball of chewing gum in his mouth. His smile seemed appropriate for any reaction, with only a small adjustment, here and there, in the corner of his lip or eye. He had probably lied as easily to Shellie not only about his name and his relationship with Mr Plute, but about how he had obtained the room because he had almost certainly obtained it fraudulently through his job at the Events Department, of which Matthew was the manager. If Tom was paying for the room, it would have cost more than his salary, which he may have been willing to pay, if only to impress Shellie with his resources, a common mating strategy among those who pay for a woman's attentions. But Tom wasn't ugly. He didn't need a show of resources to attract Shellie. Her face had sweetened as soon as he had called from the bedroom, and ever since his appearance, she had been looking at him almost exclusively, though she had also glanced at Matthew, now and then, as if to show that she hadn't forgotten him. She had to look at both of them, to preserve each in the belief that he was her preference. Maybe she hadn't expected Tom to be in the bedroom when she had invited Matthew to stay for the night. Or maybe she had planned to lure Matthew to her bed to make Tom jealous. Maybe she had only pretended to be enraged. Or maybe her rage had been real because she had been in love with Matthew since childhood, or at least since last year's spring festival, and had been planning to consummate their relationship, and though she had seen Tom sleeping naked in the bedroom, she had known that Tom could be convinced that her raging at Matthew proved that Tom was her preference. She had likewise probably expected Matthew to interpret her rage as proof that she preferred him to Tom, but he wasn't a fool. Though he was more handsome than Tom, he wasn't nearly as wealthy as Tom was pretending to be, which probably made them at least equal in Shellie's evaluation, now that she was older and more mercenary when evaluating her romantic relationships.

"I've invited Matthew to sleep on the sofa," said Shellie. "He needs to stay here tonight."

"Why?" asked Tom.

"Because I forgot what day it was," said Shellie. "I didn't know you were here."

"You're always forgetting what day it is," said Tom.

"I make mistakes sometimes," said Shellie. "And you need to accept that."

"I wouldn't have agreed to stay," said Matthew, "if I'd known the circumstances."

"But you're welcome to stay," said Tom.

"But—the circumstances," said Matthew.

"Whatever you want to do," said Tom.

"Please stay," said Shellie.

"Stay," said Tom. "That's best. By tomorrow, we'll forget this happened."

Matthew understood "we'll forget this happened" as a suggestion to forget that Tom had obtained the room fraudulently, but though Matthew couldn't be certain that Tom hadn't paid for the room, and though Matthew had more important concerns, he wasn't willing to allow Tom to believe that no consequences would follow a violation of the hotel's rules. But Matthew was also in violation of the rules merely by being in the new section of the hotel without authorization, and he was grateful for the opportunity to sleep on the sofa. He was therefore willing to ignore Tom's violation, but only if Tom avoided even the appearance that they were agreeing not to expose one another. He therefore said that "whatever had happened, if anything, he'd ignore it, this once," and he thanked them again for allowing him to sleep on the sofa. Tom received this thanks graciously. If Tom had actually been Mr Plute's nephew, he couldn't have appeared more gracious, but when he took Shellie's hand and led her into the bedroom, his smile was too relieved to be completely convincing.

20. He never uses *pair* in this context

When Matthew was finally alone on the sofa, the obligations of the next day overshadowed his thoughts of Shellie. It was comforting to think—as he unbuttoned his pants—that he had a role to perform. His absence from work had probably caused his co-workers to disseminate a rumor about him being sick, or even dead. How surprised they would be when he would show himself healthy and alive! He couldn't accept the thought that nobody had missed him. At the very least, they would have missed his work because even though his work required nothing much more than sitting, he had always done more than that, if only to fulfill the expectations he had of himself.

But after an hour, he was still lying on the sofa, unable to sleep. He was thinking about his deceased father, and about ghosts, and about the man with a mustache who had woken him from a nightmare. After a second hour, he was still lying on the sofa, unable to sleep. The darkness was around him. After a third hour, he was still lying on the sofa. He was listening to the silences in the spaces between the raindrops that were splashing against the window. The darkness was around him. After a fourth hour, he was lying on the sofa, unable to sleep. After a fifth hour, the cuckoo clocks cried out throughout the Mansion of Left Turns. It was three o'clock in the morning, as in all the children's books. The darkness was around him. After a sixth hour, he was lying on the sofa, unable to sleep. After a seventh hour, he was awake. Thunder had shaken the hotel. After an eighth hour, he was still lying on the sofa. The darkness was around him. After a ninth hour, he was still lying on the sofa. The darkness was around him.

When he woke from a sleep that he couldn't remember, it was barely morning. He was relieved that he had woken early enough to arrive at work before anyone else. He would surprise them all, assuming they had assumed him to be dead. But as he sprang from the sofa with all the vigor of his determination, he was surprised by Shellie Readling. She was sitting on a little chair that she had placed beside him, as if to examine him before feeding on his body. She had probably been the reason he had woken so suddenly, though he hadn't been aware of her. She was wearing a nightgown, and her hair had been carefully pinned aside with a golden moth.

"Matthew," she said, "I'm sorry about what happened."

"I'm sorry, too," said Matthew, though he wasn't sure why he was apologizing.

"I hate to think we've ruined everything!"

"We haven't. I promise."

Matthew didn't know what he was promising, but Shellie wilted with relief, which made him believe that he had said the correct words, even without knowing what he meant by them.

"I have to go, Shellie. I can't be late," he said.

"But it's early," said Shellie.

"I have to be early today."

He promised again that "everything wasn't ruined," but she seemed less pleased than when he had promised the first time. Maybe his intonation had sounded less confident, or maybe he had stressed the wrong words, or maybe the repetition itself had made his assertion suspicious, as if he needed to emphasize the lie so it would be believed. But he couldn't control her reactions, and he couldn't explain his feelings because he didn't know what they were. He quickly dressed and left without trying to explain why he had to be at the office before anyone else, and as soon as he was in the hallway, he was acting as if he were Bill Robbins. His sleep, though brief, had refreshed him. He felt prepared to meet Roselyn Spring. He walked slowly through the hallways, but instead of going to the office as he had intended, he went straight to his room. He planned to skip another day of work. He had always striven to be punctual and efficient. He had always desired to please his superiors. He had worked to earn the admiration of everyone. After having performed at an extraordinary level for many years, he believed he could allow himself to make one mistake.

He entered his room and went straight to his cabinet. He opened drawer after drawer. Shellie had replaced his possessions where he wouldn't have expected them, though a few of the drawers, such as the largest and the smallest, contained the same items in the same places as he had put them originally. His shoes, for example, were in a drawer below his socks, and his hats were in the same drawer as his gloves. He would need only a few days to become accustomed to the new locations of his most frequently used possessions. His infrequently used possessions, however, would require a few months, at least, before he could remember their new positions, or even find them. Roselyn's hairbrush wasn't where it had always been, and he wasn't able to locate his measuring tape, even after searching in drawers that ought to have been a good fit for it.

He was looking for the measuring tape when Roselyn Spring opened the door of his room. He was prepared for her, almost as if he had known that she would appear at that moment. Her big belly rubbed the doorframe as she entered. Her head would have seemed tiny by comparison with her body, if she hadn't been wearing a big red hat. She was looking at him with disdain. She would surely call him "Coo Coo" as usual, which she knew offended him, though she pretended it was a term of endearment. Even if he had been acting as Matthew Mathelson, he would have found her disdain intolerable, not only because a manager should be treated with respect, but because he was the father of their child, but as Bill Robbins, he returned her disdain with a contempt indistinguishable from indifference.

He was too involved in his daily concerns and in his thoughts about rectangles and books, to hate a woman who should have meant nothing to him, but who had unfortunately become the mother of his son. But if she had been anything like the illusion he had had of her when they had first met, he might have tolerated her for more than a night. Or if he had been more selfless, and therefore more easily exploited, he might have given without any expectation of a return. But despite attempts, now and then, to think about the needs of others, he thought about himself almost exclusively, and yet, despite so much thinking about himself, he didn't know himself very well.

"Hello, Coo Coo!" cried Roselyn.

Matthew was not only surprised that she sounded like a young girl, but that she could speak. She was wheezing from having walked through his doorway, and her legs, which she couldn't see beneath her bulging belly, seemed about to collapse under the weight they were being required to bear. But despite her size—or in denial of it—she was wearing dainty shoes, which made her seem like a doll that had been ballooned until she might rise off the floor and whisk through the window into the sky.

"Is Adam with you?" asked Matthew.

"He doesn't want to see you," said Roselyn.

"Why not? What have you been telling him?"

"Everything—and the truth, too."

"You're lying to him."

"No, Coo Coo, he's come to his own conclusions."

Matthew wished to end this conversation. He was already failing to act as Bill Robbins. He hadn't spoken with indifference. As Matthew, he had always been open to negotiating an agreement with Roselyn, but his offers of appeasement had earned him nothing but disrespect. If he had been reading this conversation in a book, he would have skipped it because it would have reminded him too much of the reality of his position. If Befijop had been engaged in such a conversation, he would have been disguised as a human being, which would have given the conversation an unreality that would have made it appealing. But Matthew was too much of a human being to be able to pretend to be someone he wasn't, while discussing someone as important as his son.

"I understand," he said. "You hate me. I accept that."

"You don't seem upset by it," said Roselyn, as if she

were disappointed.

"When will I see Adam?"

"He's at Aunt Demi's," said Roselyn. "He needs money for oboe lessons."

If she had looked more like the reality of what she was, Matthew would have spoken to her more effectively. But to appear as she was would have required her to appear as a fantastical image. If her hair had been pulled above her head by a school of flying fish, she would have looked an appropriately fantastical Medusa and would have therefore provided a warning to anyone foolish enough to talk with her.

"Oboe lessons!" cried Matthew. "When did Adam become interested in the oboe?"

"This winter," said Roselyn. "You should have known that. You have a responsibility to your son, Coo Coo."

"I see him as often as you allow me to see him. You never permitted me to be the father I should have been."

Matthew had been delivering money to his son for nine years, and yet, it had never been enough, not even when he was giving more than he could afford. Though Roselyn had excluded him from seeing his son, he felt guilty for not seeing him as often as he would have liked. Adam hadn't been able to understand that his mother had been a barrier that Matthew hadn't been able to overcome. Matthew hadn't been able to tell Adam what he had always wanted to tell him. He hadn't known how to say what shouldn't have had to be said, and what had to be said might have led to problems beyond what could have been expected. Matthew was unable even to say these words to himself, as if by saying them they would become the ordinary truth, instead of remaining a discomforting sense that there was a truth that he wasn't accepting. He couldn't say these words because it was impermissible to think them. Perhaps he had learned not to think them merely by means of the overwhelming weight of other people's viewpoints. He had spoken around the edges of these thoughts to strangers whom he would never see again, but even then, he hadn't been able to say precisely what was wrong; and the strangers had seemed unwilling to understand that anything had been hinted. The most significant reaction that he had obtained had been a man's laugh blown through the side of his mouth. Matthew hadn't expected anything more encouraging. He knew he had been foolish to say anything, even indirectly, but the man's laugh had implied that he, too, understood that there was a thought in the indicated direction that couldn't appear in the conversation, if they were to survive as themselves, even though much about themselves had been constructed on lies. Matthew would have done better to doubt that the pigeons had entered the hotel through a hole in the roof because such an event could be questioned among those who knew nothing about it. Or he might have discussed the various events that were happening around the world, as if it were important to have an opinion about what was happening across the ocean, and as if the reading of a few paragraphs in an article were sufficient to form an opinion that would thereafter be affirmed with passionate certainty. Such conversations were permissible because they never threatened anyone's identity directly. They were like discussions about the motives of Befijop when he lay beside the shimmering garden in the *Journey to the Lair of the Moon Golems*. Even with respect to such insignificant discussions, the participants typically felt compelled to adhere to their opinions as if adhering to themselves because if they were wrong about something as insignificant as the motives of Befijop, then they could be wrong about the things that nobody would say anything about, which would be an incomprehensible error that would result, almost, in the cancellation of themselves as people.

Roselyn was continuing to talk, but Matthew wasn't listening to her. He knew she was saying that his performance as a father had been lacking in all respects, including the amount of money he had delivered, which was—according to her—barely anything, when compared to what other children were receiving. Matthew already knew his responses to these allegations. If he would have instantly agreed to her request for money, she would have suspected he was manipulating her. He therefore denied her request, with many good reasons, forcibly expressed. She responded as he expected, by threatening to bar him from seeing his son forever. Even without listening to the discussion, which had long since escalated to a fight, Matthew was aware, merely by attending to Roselyn's intonation, that her threats had ballooned to their usual nastiness. She was willing even to invent accusations to keep him away from her son. She almost certainly wanted the money for herself because such attacks were too outlandish merely to obtain funds for Adam to learn to play the oboe, an instrument that he would discard after a month, like the clarinet and the piano, which he had abandoned as soon as the difficulty of producing even the semblance of music from them had become obvious. But regardless of her motives, Matthew was prepared to accede to her demands, or at least to appear to accede to them. He could say words as easily as she could, and they were no more meaningful to him than they were to her.

"We should stop arguing," he said, in a conciliatory tone. "But I won't bribe you—or anything like that."

"Then why won't you give me the money?"

"I'll give you the money. I want Adam to play the oboe as much as you do."

Matthew's delivery was sufficiently realistic to be convincingly sincere. Roselyn seemed to understand that he had promised as much as he would, and that any further attacks would gain her nothing more. He had apparently capitulated, even to the point of having to sacrifice for her. They exchanged a few final words, which ostensibly solidified the promise that had been made, and Roselyn turned to leave, her belly rubbing against the wall as she turned. Matthew promised once more to do everything he could, but she refused even to answer him.

21. Obviously, bluebirds can't be seen in a green tree

Matthew was relieved that Roselyn had left, but he was nevertheless upset. He was always upset after talking with her, not only because of everything that had been left unsaid about their son, but because nothing was ever resolved between them except that they would be engaged in a struggle that promised never to end until death. He would have lain on his bed; but he was too agitated to rest, and the odor of her rose perfume was floating in the room like a ghost that was determined to stay indefinitely.

He needed a reprieve where he wouldn't be thinking of her. The *Journey to the Lair of the Moon Golems* was on the pillow of his bed, where Shellie had thoughtfully placed it, possibly to convince him that she would perform similar duties if he would live with her for the rest of his days. He was relieved to see that the book hadn't been stained by Lucy's vomit. The book always intrigued him, presenting a vision of the groves on the moon, where the flowers were as tall as trees, and where the moon golems slept on sofas nesting in the blooms. His room was usually a reprieve as safe as the bloom of a gigantic flower, but to escape the lingering annoyance of Roselyn's visit, and every thought of her, he took the book and left the room to search for a quiet place to read.

He walked throughout the hotel, but though it was early in the morning, all of the lounges were occupied by at least one guest. Only the balcony beside the restaurant was vacant. Each of its nine sofas was spotted with a silver reflection of the newly risen sun. He would have preferred reading in any other place, but as if to prove that he wouldn't be bothered by memories, he sat on the sofa beside the railing, where he had once lain with Roselyn. He comforted himself with the thought that he would soon be inside the *Journey to the Lair of the Moon Golems*, but as soon as he opened the book, a shadow dropped over his shoulder like a coat. When he looked up, Roselyn was looking down at him. She was too large for him to pretend he hadn't seen her.

"When does the restaurant open?" she asked.

"You talk to me as if I'm a stranger," said Matthew.

"Don't be offended, Coo Coo."

If they had been strangers, she would have spoken to him more respectfully. If they had been strangers, he would have treated her the same as any guest at the hotel, and he would have told her when the restaurant would be open without noticing how small her head was in comparison with her body. To encounter her again at the sofa disrupted his memories. His surroundings were the same as they had been nine years before, even if the sofa was only a copy, in approximately the same position, facing the distant triangular pines, which seemed not to have grown. But when Roselyn stood before him like a character who had wandered into the performance from a different play, the surroundings seemed to have been erected for a stage on which they would caricature two lovers in a farce. When he had first met her, she had seemed as lovely as her fairytale name. He couldn't have imagined anyone more sweet, her smile like two doves looking down on a baby in a crib. She had gently rubbed the hair off his forehead, as if to bless him, as if to unite their souls. She had convinced him that love songs, which he had previously disdained, were true. She had talked to him as if they had been the only people alive, as if they knew a secret that others could never know. He had believed himself within a bubble at the tip of a magician's wand, ready to be flung into outer space. Though he had been deluded, he yet cherished the delusion and wished it to remain undefiled. It had been the most spectacular dream he had ever dreamed, and his greatest mistake. But as a result of this mistake, he had become a father, which was his great consolation. Adam was the fruit that had flowered from the miraculous moon. Matthew was always ready to come to a mutually beneficial agreement with Roselyn, respecting their son, but before he could raise the topic, she announced:

"I need to sit."

The sofa, by comparison with her bulk, was only a chair that would doubtfully bear her weight. If she had had no legs, she would have been a ball, but she couldn't have rolled herself because her arms weren't long enough to reach around her body to the ground. As she was crouching to sit beside him, her legs failed, and she dropped into the seat. Though Matthew squeezed against the armrest to give her as much room as possible, her belly pushed against him as if it were molding him. But he acted as though her belly wasn't squeezing him to the point where he almost had to gasp for air to speak.

"I want to talk about our son," he said, in a neutral voice used for opening a negotiation. "Adam needs a father. He told me he misses me."

"Oh!" Roselyn suddenly wailed, "I sit here on our sofa—and this is what you say?"

"What would you like me to say?" asked Matthew, perplexed.

"It's all misery and hopelessness!" she cried, her eyes mirroring with tears. She limply placed her hands on her belly as if on a convenient table that she always carried with her. Her fingernails were painted with gold swirls like tadpoles; they were so exquisite that Matthew suspected that they had been painted with the help of his funds.

"Tell me what's wrong," said Matthew.

"You wouldn't understand—because you hate me!"

"I never hated you."

"But you do—I know you do!"

He almost tried to comfort her by saying that he cared nothing much for her at all, and therefore couldn't hate her any more than he could hate a stranger; but he sensed that this would have been inappropriate, and also inaccurate because he wasn't as indifferent to her as he sometimes told himself. She was, at least, a person to whom he had once attached an illusion, and she was the mother of their son, which made her mental stability important.

"Have you spoken about this problem with anyone who might help you?" asked Matthew.

"Don't talk to me! It's all lies—everything!"

"It's not all lies."

"Nothing—despair! It's all a horrible delusion!"

"What's a horrible delusion?"

"You! And everything! Oh—how could you understand? Do you want to understand? Truly?"

"I do."

"But if I explained myself—would you accept me?"

"Accept you?—What do you mean?"

"Would you accept the situation as it is—as it must be?"

"I can't know until you tell me what situation you're talking about."

"I'm talking about Adam. I'm his mother. You'll never take him from me."

"And I'm his father. But I rarely see him. How can that be good for him?"

"You have your ideas, and I have mine. But I'm living in reality."

"And where am I living?"

"In a tangle inside your mind!" she cried, letting her tears drip to her chin. "But you should listen to me because I'm trying to help you!"

"How are you helping me? By excluding me from my son?"

"You can't be allowed to give him your attitudes. If you saw how determined he is to play the oboe—! How proud I am of him!"

"I'm proud of him, too."

"You say that because you think you should say that. You talk—in formulas. You talk as if you've chosen your words yesterday!"

"I probably admitted something like that to you years ago. And now, you're using this to attack me."

"Why shouldn't I use what I know against you?"

"You don't understand me, Roselyn. You truly don't understand me. I only want to be his father."

At that moment, the doors of the restaurant opened, and Roselyn bounced up like a ball from the sofa, full of eagerness to eat. She was so eager to eat—or perhaps so accustomed to treating Matthew impersonally—that she neglected to say goodbye or even acknowledge that the discussion had ended.

After she left, Matthew sat with his book, but instead of reading it, he was staring at his lap.

22. Not yet the end

Matthew's encounter with Roselyn had exhausted him. Even if he could have gone to work that day, he would have been incapable of performing adequately. But he nevertheless intended, eventually, to arrive at his office, if merely to demonstrate that he could appear even when exhausted, and he therefore returned to his room and lay in his bed fully dressed, to be ready upon waking to resume his role as a manager. But he hadn't anticipated how much sleep he would need. He had had almost no sleep on the various sofas on which he had lain for the last few nights. He slept the rest of the day and into the evening, and all through the night.

He had suspected that he would die in his bed like his father, but he was only thirty-three, which was too young to die even in a dream. He nevertheless knew that something was fatally different when Tai-yu, the heroine of the *Dream of the Red Chamber*, was brushing her hair at the foot of his bed. She was silhouetted against the white night in the window. A parrot was perched on her shoulder. The parrot was as green as other parrots, but seemed greener due to the contrast with Tai-yu's red gown, under which Matthew suspected she was hiding a machine gun, though he had no basis for this suspicion.

"Excuse me," said Matthew, pushing aside the blankets and standing from the bed. "Why are you here?"

Tai-yu refused to answer; or she might not have understood his question. But the parrot on her shoulder twisted to stare at him and said,

"*Je cherche un hôtel où l'on accepte les animaux.*"

Matthew recognized this as French, which he was surprised to hear from Tai-yu's Chinese parrot.

"Please," he said, "come another day."

But neither Tai-yu nor her parrot replied. She seemed, however, to have heard his voice because she ran behind the window curtain and came out again as St Gemma Galgani, whom Matthew recognized from a stained glass window in the church where he had been baptized. She had tied her hair into a knot at the back of her head.

"Maybe you recognize me now," said St Gemma.

"I recognize you," said Matthew, straightening his shirt and pants to look more presentable.

"We're visiting Father Abraham. Look back through the window, and see how far you've come."

The window showed a black sky with a single point of light.

"See that point?" asked St Gemma.

Matthew knew what he was seeing, and he was afraid.

"Don't be afraid," said St Gemma. "I'm often this far from the universe."

"What happened to me?" asked Matthew. "Am I dead?—But I can't be dead!"

"You won't know the details until the Last Judgment. But every story moves toward the same two words. I died when I was twenty-five. Open the cabinet if you want to see your sister."

"I had a sister?"

Matthew opened the cabinet. A drawer near the top was missing, and a woman of about his age was looking at him through the rectangular opening. Her face looked somewhat like a horse's, with a long, straight nose that she probably needed to wipe with a tissue. She had recently brushed her gleaming hair.

"You're my brother," she said. "I live in this cabinet."

"You brushed your hair with Roselyn's hairbrush," said Matthew.

"I wanted to make myself more presentable for our first meeting."

Though he was annoyed that she had used the hairbrush without his permission, he showed no annoyance because he wanted her to feel that she was part of his family, even though she was a stranger. But even if his greeting had been somewhat impersonal, she seemed incapable of being offended.

"Have you seen the angel yet?" she asked, wiping her nose.

"I'd rather not see him again," said Matthew. "He carries a machine gun."

"Would you like to see your father?"

"Yes, please."

"Look through the telescope. It's in the top left drawer of this cabinet."

"That's where I kept the measuring tape. Is there a telescope there now?"

He opened the drawer and found a small telescope. He looked through it. A great distance away, in a small room the size of a closet, his father was lying on a sofa and reading a book. He looked the same as Matthew's last memory of him, except he had a bushy beard. He must have grown the beard during the two years since he had died because it was much fuller than it had ever been, and even had wild curls that were flying into his eyes. He had been a loving father, and cheerful, and capable, and almost every other positive adjective in the thesaurus, exemplifying these attributes to the point of almost being the definition of them, but Matthew had never seen him comb his beard, which made him a believable person. He didn't want to exaggerate his father's good attributes. He would have loved him even if he had been an ordinary man, and even if he had had flaws or secrets.

"I'd like to talk to him," said Matthew.

"It's too late for that," said St Gemma, snatching the telescope from his eyes. "You have to go to work."

As soon as she said this, Matthew woke in his bed and threw the blankets off his face. It was the morning of the next day. He was again late for work, though only by a few minutes. He sprang out of bed and pulled on the green pants that had once belonged to his father. He was fully dressed in less time than a child takes to recite the alphabet.

23. He should be elsewhere

While hurrying to his office, Matthew was thinking about his sister, especially about her upper lip, which had had an odd fold when she had smiled. If she had been a female copy of himself, he could have assumed that she was nothing but a phantom from his imagination because St. Gemma Galgani had obviously stepped out of a stained glass window and his father from a memory; but he couldn't relate the fold in his sister's lip to anything of which he was aware. He had never had a sister, or at least had never known that he had had one. He would have thought about her for the rest of the day if he hadn't, on opening the door of his office, found the Restaurant Head sitting at his desk.

The Restaurant Head didn't look up when Matthew entered. Maybe the Restaurant Head couldn't move while digesting the food necessary to maintain the functioning of his huge body. He was wearing a green suit that had become too small for him; his hands and neck were bulging from it like excretions.

"Leave," said the Restaurant Head, without lifting his head. "You're interrupting me."

Matthew would have reprimanded the Restaurant Head for his impertinence, but a window—which was nothing but a rectangular opening—had recently been cut into the wall. It looked into the neighboring office, which was the Infrastructure Manager's. But the Infrastructure Manager wasn't sitting at his desk; instead, Shellie Readling was sitting at the desk, and she was wearing a shirt emblazoned with an insignia that read "Infrastructure Manager." Her hair was tied back from her face, which made her look like a different person.

"It's you," she said.

"When did you become the Infrastructure Manager?" asked Matthew.

"Yesterday," said Shellie. "Are you surprised?"

"But you wanted to become a polymer chemist."

"I never know what I'll be doing tomorrow. It's supposed to be sunny tomorrow. And I've been wanting to go for a walk."

Matthew hadn't expected her to apply to be the Infrastructure Manager, but he also hadn't known her as well as he should have. He was often surprised by what happened not only to himself, but to others, even though the managers were often being replaced. He considered developing the conversation further, perhaps even to suggest that he accompany her on her walk, but he knew his temptations too well to consider them anything other than swans that would fly away with cherries in their beaks. The pleasures of doing what he shouldn't never outweighed the serenities of doing what he should, and even under different circumstances, in a different world—even among moon golems on the moon where it might have been possible to approximate a fairy tale—he wouldn't have risked a relationship with a woman whom he was only pretending to know. He therefore congratulated her for obtaining a managerial position, and he turned back to confront the Restaurant Head, intending to command him to vacate the office.

The Restaurant Head, however, had left the desk to talk with the Head Head, who was standing outside the door. The Head Head was so tall that his head almost touched the ceiling. His shirt and pants were straight, and his hair was parted to show a straight, white line of scalp. Matthew never liked to encounter the Head Head because the Head Head demanded both the impossible and the irrelevant, without ever seeming to be aware that his demands were always ignored in practice. Everything at the hotel functioned better without the Head Head's interference, though the Head Head was, nevertheless, universally regarded as necessary. Even Matthew regarded the Head Head as necessary, if only to provide the justification for the facade that the managers were acting in concert, within a structure that gave them authority, like a clothes hanger on which a shirt acquires its form. In the presence of the Head Head, Matthew's portrayal of himself as an extraordinary manager always became like the grandiloquent final monologue of a hero in a play, a performance that was intended to stun the audience into an amazement so powerful that only silence could be the adequate response. But before Matthew could straighten his posture, the Head Head said,

"You're not supposed to be here. You've been fired."

"I've been fired?" asked Matthew, though he had not only heard the Head Head's words, but had understood them better than he had understood anything the Head Head had ever said. "But how can I be fired?"

"Because you made a mistake."

"Only one," said Matthew. "But I've always been an extraordinary manager."

"You've been demoted to Storage Attendant."

"Thank you," said Matthew. This was probably the wrong response; but he hadn't ever been demoted, and he didn't know what to say in such a situation. He sought to improve his response by adding, "I'll be the best Storage Attendant the Polka Dot Hotel has had." But this sounded not only wrong, but as insincere as an actor rehearsing an awkward line that should have been cut, though he had meant what he had said as much as he had meant anything that he had ever said to the Head Head.

The Head Head, however, seemed pleased with Matthew's response, and blinking slowly as if lulled by a melody on the piano, he instructed Matthew to descend to the storage room and obtain a sofa needed for Mr Plute's birthday party. Matthew left immediately as instructed. He was resolved to prove himself. He even expected to advance more quickly than his previous expectations, especially if the Restaurant Head proved unable to generate the results that Matthew had generated. Matthew could easily suppose that a setback was an advancement. He had read of bleak situations that were actually blessings, and he accepted that he deserved the demotion because he had been late without excuse, or at least without an excuse that management could be expected to accept. He didn't resent being treated fairly. He even considered the demotion to be evidence of the value in which he had been held because he could have just as easily been cast away. But as he descended staircase after staircase toward the storage room, he suspected that someone was playing a joke on him, and when he opened the door of the storage room, expecting the joke to be consummated, the far wall was in darkness. The storage room was enormous, and it contained a forest of sofas standing upright on their ends.

A few of the sofas near the door had been set down

on their legs. On one of these sofas, Dr Helen Nostram and Lucy Crowe were sitting beside one another.

"You were expecting me?" asked Matthew.

"How could we know you were coming?" asked Lucy.

"Why are you sitting here in the dark?" asked Matthew. "Is this a joke?"

"It's not dark," said Lucy, nodding toward a lamp on a little table beside her. She was wearing a black hat that was awry, probably because she had tugged it into a more comfortable position.

"But you seem to be expecting me," said Matthew.

"We weren't," said Lucy. "We're looking for a new sofa for the infirmary. Maybe you can help us."

"Lucy—I can't help you anymore. I'm not useful to you anymore. I've been demoted to Storage Attendant."

Dr Nostram raised her bony arm to emphasize her pronouncement: "You don't understand how things work here."

"Dr Nostram understands everything that happens here," said Lucy. "Can you keep a secret?"

"I can keep a secret," said Matthew.

"Then fold your lips together, and listen to everything Dr Nostram says."

"You weren't fired for being late," said Dr Nostram. "You were fired because you wear green pants. The Head Head wears green pants, too. He thought you were imitating him."

"He saw me as a threat?" asked Matthew, astounded.

"He saw you as an opportunist," said Dr Nostram. "Willing to please others only to advance yourself—and to hell with other people."

Matthew doubted this was true. He had rarely worn green pants to work. He owned only one pair of green pants, which he had obtained from his father's closet. He had worn them to resurrect his father in himself, or at least to feel close to him by wearing his clothing. But he couldn't discount Dr Nostram's explanation entirely. Her explanation was in line with what he could have supposed about the Head Head. Matthew had often been affected by decisions that others had made, but he hadn't always known what those decisions had been. He knew only the stories that he was telling himself about other people, based on assumptions that were probably false.

24. The sofa

The duties of the Storage Attendant hadn't been enumerated, but Matthew nevertheless assumed that he ought to know what was in the storage room. He left Lucy and Dr Nostram, excusing himself by explaining that the Head Head had given him an assignment, and he wandered through the gigantic room. He assumed he could go in any direction and reach a wall, but reaching a wall wasn't as easy as he had supposed because the forest of sofas standing upright on their ends forced him to swerve from his intended direction.

The sofas were patterned with parrots nesting in paisley sperms. Matthew couldn't conceive why so many sofas had been acquired. Obviously, the number of them was excessive; otherwise, they would have been placed throughout the hotel instead of being buried in the storage room, where they were becoming musty and moth-eaten. But Matthew was the Storage Attendant, not the Infrastructure Manager, and he shouldn't have been worrying about what wasn't his responsibility. If he had been a parrot instead of a parent, he could have said the same words over and over while still being amusing, but he needed now to be only what he was, with all his characteristics, which included his limitations.

When he came upon a sofa that had been knocked over onto its legs, he didn't notice it until he bumped it with his knee. As soon as he was lying on it, he realized how sleepy he was. He had apparently been sustained until that moment by his anxiousness to perform adequately in his new role. He resolved to say something in the Restaurant Head's favor at the next opportunity, not only to show others that he didn't resent being demoted, but to prove it to himself. He had finally escaped the need to be important in the opinions of other people.

While lying on the sofa, he wasn't aware of dreaming anything, and he wasn't even aware of being asleep, though he assumed he must have been, afterward. When he woke, the storage room looked exactly the same, except a man with a twitching mustache was standing over him. Matthew had seen this man now and then, doing small jobs—of various kinds—for the hotel, but he had never noticed what should have been apparent from the beginning.

"You look like a ghost," said the man. "Have I frightened you?"

"I thought I was alone," said Matthew.

"No, I'm here, too."

"Now that you're here, maybe you can help me."

"What do you need?" asked the man with the mustache. "I'll do anything if it's easy."

"Help me carry this sofa to the balcony. It's needed for Mr Plute's birthday party."

The man unbuttoned his shirt to increase the mobility of his arms, which would be useful for carrying the sofa up many staircases; but by unbuttoning his shirt, he revealed a green bodysuit beneath it, the same bodysuit that Befijop had worn beneath his disguise in the *Journey to the Lair of the Moon Golems*. Maybe the man was a moon golem, but Matthew was grateful to have his help, even without knowing who he was.

Matthew lifted one end of the sofa, and the man lifted the other end. They bore the sofa out of the storage room and maneuvered it up many staircases to the balcony. As soon as the sofa was positioned near the railing, Matthew suspected that it was the same sofa on which he had lain with Roselyn Spring, nine years before. But all of the sofas at the hotel were identical.

Matthew thanked the man for his help, but the man twitched as if he had found the thanks humorous, or at least inappropriate. His mustache also twitched.

It was late in the evening, and Mr Plute's birthday party had already begun in the restaurant adjoining the balcony. In the restaurant, the tables had been pushed to the walls, presumably to clear a space for dancing. The guests were dressed in their best clothes as if for their graves. The man with the mustache joined the party. He greeted a woman who appeared to be Shellie Readling, though a floppy hat hid her face, and then he descended a staircase. If Matthew could have remained unseen, he might have escaped everyone's memory. He would have lain on the sofa by the railing, if it wouldn't have reminded him of Roselyn Spring, but despite his desire never to see her again, she came out on the balcony. Her face was dripping with tears. She was hurrying to fling herself facedown on a sofa, or at least drop herself because she was too fat to fling herself easily, and also dropping was more dramatic, and therefore preferable. She was obviously acting in her own drama, which probably involved failing to attract Mr Plute, with whom she imagined she had a romantic relationship, but when she saw Matthew Mathelson, a curtain dropped across her stage. Her distress was as if wiped off her face with a napkin, probably with a rectangular napkin because not only were most napkins rectangular, but everything about Roselyn was contrived, though she lived among rectangles without being aware of them. She was wearing a gold gown and as many cheap gems as she could hang on herself.

"Is Adam with you?" she asked.

"Who?" asked Matthew. "Adam?—My son?"

"Who else, Coo Coo?—I'm sorry to call you that, but you really are cuckoo sometimes.—Is he with you?"

"Should he be?"

Adam must have heard them talking about him. As if responding to their summons, he appeared in the field below the balcony. The boy was carrying a pear that he had probably found in the pear grove. He was walking beside the man with a mustache. Maybe Matthew had been distracted by the mustache, which had often been twitching, and therefore hadn't noticed what should have been apparent from the beginning. The man looked the same as Adam. Even the man's chin was the same as the boy's. It would have been obvious that they were father and son, if it hadn't been so unbearable.

"What strange things have happened to me," thought Matthew, "but it was all so ordinary."

The End